Existence and Other Stories

Bill Wahl

ISBN: 978-1-326-43655-1

PublishNation, London
www.publishnation.co.uk

Also by Bill Wahl

The Art of Impossibility
(a novel)

CONTENTS

Disappear

I'd never witnessed a car accident before. I'd driven past them after the event – you know – dented metal, broken glass and flares on the road, police directing traffic, some despondent individual speaking into a phone and waving their arms about. But this was the first time I'd actually seen one happen. Not that what I witnessed was much of an accident, but that's really beside the point.

I'm sitting in the café of this huge Barns & Noble bookstore. Perching on one of those tall stools, I face a long table and stare out a large window, my back to the café clientele. The interesting thing about the long table is that it affords the possibility of strangers sitting next to one another. To my right is a young man glowing with health, industriously glued to a laptop computer. To my left is a pretty college girl wearing a pink sweatshirt that reads *Martha's Vineyard*. She pokes at an iPhone while fingering an Oprah book of the month. Behind me, dozens of conversations collide indiscernibly, mixed with smells of strong coffee and gourmet chocolate cookies.

Gliding ghostlike through falling snow, I notice a glossy red SUV moving slowly from left to right. I can see the woman driver. At the same time, I see a man in a silver Mercedes sedan drive leisurely in a lane towards me and proceed to turn left across the path of the SUV. Neither driver touches their brakes before the woman's shiny chrome fender makes a dull metallic thudding contact with the Mercedes' rear panel. It's all slow-motion, and I take in details of the cars, drivers, and gawking pedestrians in surprising detail. Both cars come to an abrupt stop, and for a dreamlike moment nothing happens. I mean the world goes on as before – the café bubbles with conversation, shoppers browse and push their way about nicely, people frown as they wait in lines, overpriced coffee beans picked by dark unknown people are crushed and steamed and sniffed. The industrious young man and the pretty Martha's Vineyard girl have seen (or perhaps heard) what happened. They look around me and briefly make eye contact. They have never met one another, but seem to know instinctively that they should look *around me* and acknowledge what happened with each other. Nevertheless, they shrug the accident off, returning attention largely to their computer and book. But I know better. The routine and ritual of our local universe has been disturbed. This is not to be missed.

The man and woman remain in their cars for a moment, and as I wait, I find myself attending to the snow. To begin with, I think I saw *snow* falling. But I seem to know just now that it is really individual snowflakes falling – falling in their countless numbers and in their silent, unassuming way. The pavement of the parking lot is wet, and each snowflake disappears completely the instant it reaches the sodden blackness. I imagine that it will not take long for the individual flakes to gather and create a snowy blanket on the hardness of the asphalt. But the curious thing is that this does not happen – the seeming billions of separate flakes hit and vanish and the repetition occurs over and over.

The man and women emerge from their cars simultaneously, as if an unseen ball has been hiked and they have been sent forward. But these players go into action in a careful, measured manner, meeting out roles which, strangely, they seem to know already. She is in her middle forties, attractive, well-kept, and wearing a long mustard-yellow wool coat. He is perhaps ten years older, silver hair, black leather driving gloves emerging from another long wool coat (is it dark blue or black?). I'd say he was a doctor – some sort of specialist. They move with feigned congeniality to a physical proximity which is probably conventional for most cocktail parties, and begin to discuss the unhappy event. The uproar of conversation, tepid Christmas music, and spitting espresso machine consigns the scene beyond the window to silence.

As I look on, I suddenly sense myself as hollow and not-here-ness – a bit floaty even. It could be this regime of medication I have to take, but I've just come from the University so it could be the beer as well. I know, part-time adjunct professors should *not* drink two cans of beer just prior to teaching their 3:00 PM Abnormal Psychology class. They shouldn't do it because it's wrong. Yet this is a little ritual I fell into six months ago. At the time I had received some really bad news about my health just hours before one of my afternoon classes, and I was confused and scared and angry and I put two cans of beer in my canvass bag with my textbook and lecture notes, which, strangely, seemed like the thing to do. Arriving an hour before my class, I wanted to find a safe place to drink those beers. I share the Adjunct Office with four other professors, but they're rarely in so I figured I would drink the beer there. Just my luck, one of the other flunkies was using it. No matter, I sat in a nearby bathroom stall and sipped slowly at those cans like an infant at his mother's soft breast. And it helped a little bit. Around the stall I could hear staff and students urinating, washing hands, exchanging superficial pleasantries, opening and closing doors – and all the while I held the coolness of the can to my lips, trying not to think. Scrawled onto the stall walls was the usual repulsive and regressive messages, honest despite their awfulness – and I felt at home there. A teacher of Abnormal Psychology sits in a bathroom stall drinking beer before his class and contemplating profanity – the irony was not lost on me. I even continued to choose the peculiar suitability of the bathroom stall over the adjunct office. Of course it's wrong for a professor to drink before his classes. But what do you want me to do? Talk to a caring professional who can offer me unconditional positive regard and empathize accurately with my feelings? Screw that.

Things are *not* going so well for the attractive woman and doctor. The mutual pleasantness, warm smiles, and easy body movements have given way to something quite different. Expressions have become reciprocally stony, bodies rigid, words serious. And just now, small flashes of anger and pointing to the scene of discontent. Oh dear.

Rising from the din of affability behind me, I hear two women chatting. I noticed them when I came in – middle age, plenty of make-up, jewelry glinting, hairdos rigid and glistening. One of them has apparently left her husband (finally!) and has had a date. The date and new man is being dissected in remarkable detail. Words come rushing out with force and enthusiasm, neither woman seeming to finish a thought before the other woman begins a new avenue of appraisal. I don't know, maybe that's how it's supposed to be done. The espresso machine gushes loudly to my left, spewing air and hot milk. A ringing joins the happy melee, and the pretty Martha's Vineyard girl answers her phone. She becomes animated, intimate, and coy and I am certain she speaks with a muscled boyfriend with a solid, square jaw. My watch beeps suddenly, reminding me to take my medication. I don't want to abandon my observation of the mysterious happening beyond the window, but I know from experience that if I don't take my meds straight away I'm liable to forget.

Even under my long-sleeve shirt and jeans, I feel my limbs poking out into this café land of nourished beings as I work my way to the drinking fountain. I feel so skinny – all elbows and knees inclining at awkward angles, sure to catch a counter top or corner. I take my meds and totter back towards my stool, a figure Giacometti might look upon with a knowing grin. On route, I pass a display of those companion booklets which help you understand

4

classic novels. I've been considering reading James Joyce's *Ulysses,* but it's an awfully thick book and I'll probably have to read it slowly so I don't lose track of the plot or get the characters muddled up. I'm worried I won't have time to finish the book before... well, things get bad, so I consider getting one of these guides to help me. The booklet for *Ulysses* is there and beneath the title it reads **Smarter, Better, Faster**, which sounds like what I need, but a haze of lethargy tugs at me and I decide against it.

As I climb back onto my stool, I notice that things beyond the window have deteriorated yet further. The attractive woman is holding her arms wide and is shouting in exasperation as if trying to explain something simple to a dull child or foreigner. The individual flakes continue to fall around them, disappearing into the wet blackness, and for reasons I don't understand (the beer? the medication?) the falling flakes have a hypnotic effect on me. There is something important about the snowflakes, but the truth of the thing is content to grin silently at me. And I grin in return because this is just as it should be. I wasn't always this way. No – the universe was elegant and sensible, and I was one of those social scientists creating all that elegance and sensibility. I researched and tapped feverishly at my computer, and all that cosmic messiness seemed to get sorted right out! What conceit. Comprehending and doing, comprehending and doing – it used to be like a mantra whispering its way through my days. Not anymore. Now I am like a snake that lies stiff and immobile, blood frozen, thankful for fickle moments of warmth – moments where the incomprehension of it all, delivered to me through chance events, holds me close like a lover. I traded in Newton for a Magritte painting – traded in the self-importance of comprehension for the mystery behind it all.

The unhappy accident victims are not making any progress, and I notice a few cars lined up behind their stricken vehicles. I sense quite suddenly that I might lose an opportunity. Something tips over inside of me and I abandon my stool, grab my jacket, and make for the doors. The attractive woman and could-be doctor do not acknowledge my presence at first, so I stand next to them like a third cocktail party guest eager to join their conversation. I realize immediately that neither wishes to pause to consider this new guest out of fear that the other might get in *a last word*. They have definitely put aside all car accident etiquette.

"You pulled out directly in front of me. It's your responsibility to stop, but you drove into my path..." the woman says.

"Excuse me, there is no stop sign. I am no more responsible for stopping than you are, and the fact of the matter is that *you* hit me. It's your front fender sticking into the side of my car..."

I realize that I could be standing here, unacknowledged, for some time to come, so I interrupt as politely as I can.

"Pardon me. I don't mean to stick my nose into other people's business, but I did in fact clearly see the accident from the window (I point behind me). If you feel you need a witness, I'd be pleased to help."

For a moment they stare at me, surprised and stuck for a response. Something pleases me about their stuckness, and I manage to offer a serious and concerned expression, though it's necessary to suppress a giggle forming at the base of my bowel. The sound of a car horn pushes itself abruptly into the space where we have suspended conversation, and I realize that a new feature of this mysterious happening has made itself known. The line of blocked cars has grown, and some anonymous and impatient consumer has felt compelled to use his horn.

"Yes... a witness," the well-kept woman says. "I think that's a good idea."

"Yes, I agree, obviously," the specialist concurs. "But we need to move our cars," he adds, motioning to the waiting drivers.

"Look," I say. "Why don't you park your cars and then meet me in the bookstore café.

This is reasonable to all, so we temporarily go our separate ways. Entering the bookstore, it suddenly occurs to me how unlikely it is that we will find a table which is free. But as I pass into the café I notice a party of three leaving a table, which I make a beeline for. How lovely – my need and opportunity meeting and holding hands without a word said, and all for reasons which are blind and ignorant. I settle into my seat and get a feel of my new surroundings. It's three weeks to Christmas and a quiet, unacknowledged panic simmers – I saw it earlier in the superficially polite manner people steered their way around the overcrowded parking lot; I see it now in the sour expression on the face of the woman asking, *if I'm just picking up books I have on order, do I need to wait in line?* It can't be missed in the way cashmere pushes against camel hair ever so nicely and with congenial words of repentance, but pushes nevertheless. I look out the window and notice that the Doctor has managed to park the Mercedes right out front, and I can clearly make out the dull dent in the rear panel.

I am joined by my new acquaintances, neither of whom chooses to remove their jackets. I've got my jacket stowed nicely on the back of my chair. I'm comfortable, and why not? I'm the witness.

"I could go for a coffee, but the line is so long," the well-kept woman begins.

"Well, I'd really like to get on with it anyway," the Specialist says.

"Fine," the woman returns sharply.

Interesting exchange. It seems to be about whether or not to get coffee and when to start, but it's not. It's really about who's going to be in control. Coffee and the starting time are simply props.

"Okay, so what was your view of things," the Doctor asks politely.

I notice the politeness in his voice, which I like. I'm not impressed by it, but I like it.

"Well, there isn't any stop sign at the intersection where your cars met, so I imagine that it would be up to the two drivers to just decide which car went first."

"That's just what I was saying," the Doctor interrupts. "It's no more my responsibility to stop that it is hers."

The attractive woman is about to jump in, but I am not willing to let these two run amuck.

"If I can just continue, please."

"Yes, of course," the polite Doctor says.

I look over at the woman. "Ma'am, you were speaking on your portable phone (*those phones are called something else, damn it!*). You were preoccupied with your call – I could see it in your expression."

The woman's face becomes hard with dislike as she stares at me and I sense instantly that she is deciding whether to lie about the phone or minimize its importance.

"I... yes I was using a phone, but I saw him driving along on my left and I assumed it was his responsibility to stop. I still believe, cell phone or not (*that's what they're called!*) that it was his responsibility to stop."

"Hold on," the Doctor says. "There's no issue about who's responsible here. I have a witness saying that you were preoccupied with a cell phone call while you ran into my car. You are clearly at fault."

The Doctor and I wait for the attractive woman to speak, but she glares for a moment, eyes shifting between us, and then picks her purse up off the floor. She scrawls something on a napkin and pushes it forward.

"You have my insurance details," she says to the Doctor. "I'm leaving."

As she reaches for her coat I say, "but I haven't finished yet."

She freezes for a moment, and perhaps noticing the slender expression of apprehension on the doctor's face, sits down again. I continue.

"There was a young woman, a teenager I imagine, who was wearing extremely tight-fitting blue jeans wrapped around a very pretty ass. A few moments before your collision, I noticed her and her parents getting out of their car. She was walking towards the bookstore as you (I look at the Doctor) were approaching. When you turned your wheel, your head turned too and you never took your eyes off that ass. Not, of course, until you heard a bump."

The woman bursts out laughing and grins. I am not a coarse person – just the opposite, really. My words concerning the teenager were chosen carefully and for effect. The doctor didn't stop to decide whether to lie or not. He just lied.

"This is ridiculous. I didn't see any young woman. You've clearly made a mistake. All of this is beside the point. Cell phones and young women notwithstanding, you ran into the back of my car."

"Not the back of your car – the side of your car. And no, it's not beside the point. I am not paying to fix your car when you were looking…"

They argue much as they had done in the parking lot before my arrival, though now with new material for consideration – but I am feeling tired. I get tired by late afternoon – a side effect of my meds. Even though their words go out of focus, I get a vibration of what it all means. Feeling suddenly irritated with them, I interrupt.

"Look, sometimes bad things happen. We don't want them to, but they do anyways. Do you know what I think? I think people want to be in control. It's not a bad thing, really. It's quite human if you think about it. We take a shower one morning and feel about in places we have felt thousands of times before and we notice that we have a little bump in our testicle and suddenly we don't feel so much in control as we did. And that's really upsetting, you know. You used to have a Mercedes sedan which looked really great, at least from your point of view, and now it has a little bump in its ass. You (I look at the attractive woman) didn't have to think about the possibility that your insurance premiums will go up, and now you do. And you feel just that little bit less in control of your life. And it's upsetting, isn't it?"

Doctor and attractive woman are taken aback by my speech, and I'm a little surprised by it too.

"Look," says the Doctor, "I don't mean to be rude" (gosh, he's polite), "but I'm just not sure how relevant that is."

I've never hit anyone in my life and I'm quite certain I never will. But I have an image of hitting him just then. Really smacking him right in the center of his mildly annoyed and yet somehow sympathetic face. I can't look at him anymore, so I squeeze my lips together and turn my head and stare out the window. My eyes land almost immediately on his Mercedes and that inward mound of dented silver. I can hear the woman and doctor speaking again, but their voices and the seeming millions of voices around us sound very far away, as if everyone is shouting at the bottom of the darkest sea. And then, just when I want to give up on this absurd project, something occurs to me.

"You know what?" I interrupt with enthusiasm. "I've got a really good idea."

They look at me quizzically, not sure if they want to participate. No doubt they think I'm quite strange by this point.

"Come on, this will just take a minute," I say.

I put on my jacket and walk for the door, my bemused guests protesting but following me anyway. Leading them to the Mercedes, we stand together at the trunk, flakes of snow falling

10

around us and transforming into a cold wetness as they land on our faces. I take notice of the indentation. It is bowl-shaped and no paint has come off. I look at the Doctor.

"Can you open the trunk?"

He looks at the woman, and the two of them seem to communicate something between them through their expressions – perhaps a shared acknowledgment that I am an idiot. The Doctor grins as if to say, *I might as well – it can't get much nuttier than this.*

Pushing a button on his key ring, the trunk glides upward with German meticulousness. His trunk is remarkably clean and empty. We have three young children, so the sight of a really clean and empty trunk surprises me.

Sticking my head down into the trunk, I note that the dented panel is exactly the same on the inside, just reversed into a bowl rounding outward at me.

"Well, you've got a dent alright," I say, my voice sounding echoey down in the trunk.

"I thought that part was clear," I hear the woman say.

I stand up and look the two of them in the eyes. I know that what I'm about to do is crazy and I think about putting one of my winter gloves on, but I don't for reasons which I'm sure make no sense. I lean down into the trunk again and find myself just staring at that inward dent, and then all at once something is releasing in me and I'm losing control – my heart is pounding, lungs pumping, and throat constricting into a painful knot. I am squeezing my eyes tight and the muscles in my face and arms tighten into an angry and frightened spring and the hot thickness in my chest is starting to come out as tears so I open my eyes and scream and punch that dent as hard as I can.

There's quite a loud "bang" and that inner mound of a dent just pops right out. I push myself up from the trunk and the three of us inspect the panel – it's as smooth and unblemished as the day the car left the factory. And my fist hurts, but I don't want to look down at it. The faces of the woman and doctor hang before me, speechless and amazed, and they even seem a little afraid of this madman standing in front them.

"There you go," I announce. "Problem solved!" I spread my arms wide and offer them a small bow.

My tall chair is empty when I re-enter the café, so I climb on up. I'm meant to face my window, you know – not stare into the store. But I turn around and look at the happy, chatting café patrons and then beyond to the consumers who squeeze their way endlessly around the table-top displays of "thought-provoking and heart-warming" novels or self-help books which *tell you how to do it*. I feel what I know is a senseless impulse to address all of them but I am very tired and I don't really know what to say and I think there is still some capacity in me to feel embarrassment, so I face my window again and place my chin on my folded hands, elbows outward, ignoring the pain in my fingers. On my left the Martha's Vineyard girl reads purposefully and on my right the healthy young man taps at his laptop for reasons which are no doubt meaningful for him. Though they convey no interest in me, I must appear strange to them and others, for I am meant to read, sip coffee, and nibble gourmet cookies happily. But instead, a thick ball of disgust is growing inside me. I don't want to hate, but it seems I can't help it today.

Looking out the window, I gaze at the individual flakes falling quietly and without protest, disappearing again and again into the blackness of the wet pavement.

Delivery Boy, 1982

Coming up with stupid ideas and then acting on them seems to be something I'm especially good at. But what really gets me isn't that I have these ideas or even that I try to go through with them. What really gets me is that just as the idea pops into my head there's usually this sensation I have that it's all going to end badly. And what *really* gets me is that I never pay it much attention until maybe later – I mean later when everything's in the crapper. All of which reminds me to tell you about Sally.

The first time I saw Sally was on the late bus coming home from school. Sally goes to the local high school whereas I get bussed across town every day so that I can be indoctrinated by Jesuits. I get picked up from my private school around 5:00 PM on account of playing on the high school tennis team and then dropped at Sally's school about 5:30 PM, where we get onto the same bus that takes us home. I watch Sally for a few days, snatching the odd glance over my radio control catalog. She's what other people call *bubbly* – real happy in a bouncy sort of way. Shiny black Dorothy Hamell hair which is popular on account of that ice skater. Everything about Sally is rounded, but in a way I like. Rounded face, tummy, boobs, bottom. She's short, and some might say plump. But she's not fat, just real solid. To me, all that roundedness is just fine the way it moves beneath her sweaters and jeans. She always sits in her own seat, but much of the time talks to others around her, getting quite excited and smiling everywhere. Something about Sally screams *I'm a good Catholic girl who gets excellent grades and is never in trouble – a real nice, responsible girl.* You could almost be positive at the start that she would not let you have sex with her. Maybe a little groping, but she'd have her hand on my wrist the moment it tried to go south of the equator. I've been there once or twice. I know the drill. Deep down I probably want a wayward, rebellious girl with loose morals who dresses in black and swears a lot. But you don't often find that sort, and the truth is I'm scared of those girls. Besides, what would they want with me anyway – I'm a nice boy from a good home, and I'm not sure I know how to be much different. So it's Sally I watch on the late bus, wondering how I can get her to go out with me. It's Sally I watch because she's the sort of girl I know something about.

What I'm mostly trying to figure out is how to start up a conversation. It's got to be natural and spontaneous – not as if I'd spent three late bus trips turning it over in my mind. About a year ago I stumbled onto Dale Carnegie's *How to Win Friends and Influence People* at the mall bookstore. I recall glancing all around when I handed the book to the cashier – I mean, I felt like I was buying a Playboy magazine. I'd known for some time that I was on the road to Loserville, and if a book could save me, I'd risk buying the thing. Carnegie had these six principles for making people like you, and I got to admit they sure did open my eyes. I think about all the bullshit I'd been taught over the years, and it's amazing no one bothered to tell me this stuff. Principle four, encourage others to talk about themselves, seemed just what was called for.

I knew that Sally had to be in the stage band because she always kept this clarinet case nestled against her thigh. That clarinet case was my meal ticket. I waited until she happened to look over, and then cool as I could manage:

"So you play the clarinet?"

Genius, huh?

That bubbliness spilled all over me and the last five minutes before she got off the bus was pretty easy conversation. That was a Tuesday.

Later that evening I made a little list of topics we could talk about. Our schools, teachers, music we like, if we're going to college. Conversation went well on Wednesday and Thursday. Carnegie would have been pleased. My big break came on Friday. I was talking with this guy named Leonard just as theology class was about to start.

"You know Sally from the late bus?" says Leonard.

"Yeah," I answer, as if it doesn't mean much, but I can feel my chest pump harder.

"Well, she's friends with my sister, and my sister told me that Sally told her that she likes you."

"Really," I say, and my cool exterior slips a little.

But suddenly I'm only 95% sure Leonard meant that Sally likes me, rather than his sister likes me. I'd rather be run over backward by a lawn mower than make it with Leonard's sister, so I have to ask.

"Leonard, did you mean it was Sally who likes me?"

"Yea, it's Sally who likes you."

"And she said that to your sister?"

"Yea, dumb-ass. Sally told my sister she likes you."

So I'm feeling pretty confident and excited as I'm chatting with Sally on the late bus that evening. She's saying something about her chemistry class when I notice a girl a few seats forward gnawing those heart-shaped Valentines candies. That's when it occurs to me that this Saturday is Valentine's Day.

Saturday morning I ask mom if I can borrow the family Ford, telling her that I need to go to the mall to get dad a birthday present. She agrees, but Ricky, my younger brother, overhears and asks if he can come along. I'm a bit uneasy, but I can't think of a reason to say no. It's a bright, crisp sunny day as Ricky and I head into town.

"I thought you said we were going to the mall," Ricky finally says.

"Change of plans," I say. I'll admit I'm enjoying the intrigue.

"Where we going then?" Ricky asks carelessly.

"To a florist shop."

"You gonna buy Dad some flowers for his birthday?"

It's a good joke and we both laugh. We roll on in silence for a few minutes.

Finally Ricky says, "you know those people who develop rock bands, I mean the ones who come up with the idea for a band."

"Like a band promoter," I venture.

"Yeah, like that. Well if I was a band promoter I've got a great idea for a band. It's got five girls in it. Four of them are topless and play drum sets real loud all at once and the fifth girl just screams into a microphone and every song sounds almost the same."

"Is the girl who screams into the microphone topless too?" I ask.

"No," Ricky says.

"Why not?"

"Because she's not a drummer," Ricky replies, as if the point were completely obvious. "Look," Ricky continues, "the best part of it is that the band is called Vaginismus."

"Vaginismus?" I ask.

"Yea, the book we use in my sex ed class has got a list of other books in it and I thought the other books might have photos in them instead of just the medical drawings, so I got one out from the library and there was a chapter on what they call sexual dysfunctions – you know, like when your dick won't work. Anyway, I read that some women have got what's called vaginismus. You won't believe this. If you can get it into them,

16

they freak out and clamp down on you so hard that you can't even get it out again. So the idea is that you've got these four girls crashing away on drum sets and one screaming – and they're called Vaginismus!"

Ricky's very excited about this idea and I have to admit it's a pretty good one. Weird, but good.

"So what does the guy do then – I mean to get his dick out."

"The book didn't explain about that."

And that's when we pull up at the florists.

A bell tinkles on the way in and we get blasted by this moist flowery odor. The place is crammed with flowers and plants, and I'm overwhelmed immediately. I don't much like the fact that we're the only ones in the shop, and there's this antique behind the counter staring at us over the top of these low riding glasses she's got perched at the end of her nose.

"May I help you gentlemen?"

I figure it's better to ask her for help than just wander around in this maze, so I approach the counter with Ricky on my heels.

"I'd like to get some flowers... it's for a girl... you know, for Valentine's Day."

I've only got ten bucks in my wallet, so I add, "it doesn't have to be anything too fancy."

"Well, we do a basic Valentine's Day bouquet which includes an assortment of orchids, tulips, and chrysanthemums." She hobbles over to this glass cooler and pulls out what I guess is meant to be an example. It looks pretty nice, I guess.

"Uhm... how much is that?"

"The basic bouquet is $18.50."

The bell tinkles again and glancing over I can see that a businessman in a suit has made his way in. The florist is looking pretty impatient now, standing there displaying this bunch of flowers I can't afford. My impulse is to just say no thank you and head for the door, but I suddenly remember that my sister was once given roses by some guy and she practically peed herself. I overheard her on the phone to a friend, going on and on about how they were a dozen long stem roses. Maybe roses are the sort of thing you give for Valentine's Day.

"Uhm, if I got a few red roses – how much would that be?"

"You just want red roses on their own?" She's got this puzzled expression on her face, and I'm getting the impression that you're not supposed to get red roses *on their own*. Out of the corner of my eye I notice that the suit is standing at the counter and he's making this shuffling noise with one of his shoes on the floorboards.

Just then I hear Ricky from across the room say, "hey, why don't you get her one of these?" He's pointing to this massive pot that's got something in it which looks like a short palm tree that's been stuck onto the top of a deformed purple pumpkin.

The florist's lips tighten, and then she says "red roses are three dollars a piece, and I could put some greenery with them and wrap them for you – would that be okay?" I have no idea what greenery means but I can handle nine bucks, so I say that's just fine and we head for the counter. Her bony hands are covered by loose skin and age spots, but they move faster that a Las Vegas card dealer as she wraps the roses and greenery. The flowers look pretty nice, but just when it seems like everything's going well, she says something which hits me like a hammer blow to the forehead.

"Now then, would you like to have the flowers delivered?"

My jaw drops open, and all I can do is stare. I hadn't thought about having the flowers delivered. I hadn't even thought about how the flowers were supposed to get to Sally.

"Uhm, you mean you could deliver the flowers for me?" The businessman is eyeing me now, and I imagine he thinks I'm retarded.

"That's right, sir. Delivery is $7.50."

18

I glance over at Ricky, wondering if he's got any money on him, but I'm pretty sure he hasn't and I don't want to ask at this point. I just want to get the hell out of here.

So Ricky and I are sitting in the florist parking lot and I'm staring down at these roses wrapped up in green tissue paper, wondering how I'm gonna get them to Sally. I can't drive there and just hand them to her on the doorstep. I'm sure that's not right and I don't want to be there when she gets them anyway. I can't figure out what to do so I pull out this little card with a string on it which came with the flowers and think over what I want to write.

Dear Sally, happy Valentine's Day. It's been great meeting you on the bus.

It seems just right. Simple and not too mushy. Leaving my name off adds some mystery (though not much), and if Leonard is full of shit and Sally doesn't like me I can try and deny sending them. But how do I get them to her? I look over at Ricky. He's humming some song, feet up on the dash, sneakers pumping to the rhythm, staring out the window.

And that's when the idea pops into my head.

Ricky might only be 15, put he could pass for 16. Mom's Ford doesn't have a florist shop sign on the side, but I'll bet that some florist shops just deliver in plain old cars.

"Hey Ricky, how'd you like to be a florist delivery boy?"

"You want me to deliver these flowers to your new girlfriend?"

"Her name's Sally and she's not my girlfriend – just someone I met on the late bus."

"What? You gonna drive me to her neighborhood and you want me to walk the flowers to her house?"

"Well, not exactly," I say. "I don't think florists deliver on foot to the middle of suburbia, and I don't want Sally to think I'm too cheap to buy delivery."

"But you are too cheap to buy delivery."

"Ricky, the thing is I gotta get these flowers to Sally, and I want it to look like I did it the right way."

"So you gonna pull into her driveway and then I walk the flowers up to her door?"

"I'll get spotted behind the wheel. I could duck down, but if I try ducking down and get spotted, that's even worse."

I leave things in silence for a moment and I can see Ricky's turning it all over in his mind, staring at his sneakers. And then the light goes on.

"You want me to drive the car? I get to drive the car!" Ricky says with sudden excitement.

"You'd only have to drive a short distance but you'd have to act like a real delivery boy – do you think you could do it?"

"Sure," says Ricky. "But you'd have to tell me how to drive. I mean I learned some stuff from watching, but you'd have to tell me other stuff."

On route I take a closer look at Ricky and realize we've got a problem. He's wearing a grimy baseball cap and a t-shirt which reads, ASK ME IF I GIVE A SHIT. The shirt seems odd on Ricky because he's actually a really nice kid. It's just that last March we all went to Myrtle Beach and Dad gave each of us ten bucks to spend on whatever we wanted. We must have gone in and out of five gift shops. A world of plastic novelties to choose from, but Ricky just had to have that t-shirt.

"Ricky, when we get to the neighborhood, do you think we could swap shirts?"

Ricky looks down at the scrolly gold lettering on his t-shirt and gives me a big grin.

"Hey, what's wrong with my t-shirt?"

"Well, I don't think ASK ME IF I GIVE A SHIT is the sort of slogan most florists want to use. And maybe you could leave the baseball cap in the car – you look like a grease monkey."

Sally lives in a nice normal suburb which has been bolted onto a middle-sized, ordinary city. About 100 yards off a main road, Sally's neighborhood street bends to the left, and she lives just around the corner on the left side of the road. I pull onto her street and park immediately.

Mom's Ford is an automatic shift, which makes things a whole lot easier. I talk Ricky through forward, neutral, reverse, turning, accelerating, braking. Ricky's paying close attention and he looks slightly worried, but I go through everything about three times and reassure him a lot. And then we work the script up.

"So what are you going to say then?"

"Good afternoon, I have a flower delivery for Sally."

"Almost," I say. "It's good afternoon, I have a *floral* delivery for Sally."

We swap shirts and I think Ricky's ready. Scanning the street ahead, I notice there's a thick hedge on the right side of the street, just where the road starts to bend. The street is empty from what I can see and it looks like people who live in the house with the hedge are away because the garage door is closed and the curtains drawn.

"Ricky, I'm gonna be behind that hedge so I'll be able to keep watch just in case there's any problems, okay?"

"Alright," says Ricky, but he's scanning around the controls and trying the brake.

I feel a bit like a moronic commando as I make my way across and up the street, walking quickly, hunching over slightly. When I'm safely behind the hedge I notice that I've got a great side-view of Sally's driveway and front entranceway. There's a big tree behind me and so I'm completely shaded from the direct sunlight, which is everywhere. The neighborhood is pretty quiet.

21

Farther up the street some kids are playing basketball and further still some guy is mowing his lawn. Ricky hasn't moved yet. He's looking around, turning the wheel a bit, doing some last minute practice. I'd left the motor running for him and I can just make out the low hum of the pistons.

Come on Ricky, just ease the shift back into drive and let it roll.

I'm suddenly struck by how bright everything is – there's a glare off the green Ford which is so intense I have to shift my view just to be able to see Ricky. Suddenly the wheels are moving, but Ricky's still looking down! A few seconds later his head shoots up... and he's doing fine. The Ford is moving in a nice straight line, inching along at about 2 miles an hour. I can tell Ricky's just rolling in drive – he hasn't touched the accelerator. My heart is pumping hard and I can feel the blood pulsing through my throat. At first I'm pleased that Ricky's just letting her roll, but then I'm not so sure. My mind is racing. Staying off the accelerator is playing it nice and safe, but if he drives like this all the way he's going to look like a demented senior citizen to anyone who might be looking out their window. Watching Ricky, I realize that experienced drivers do everything with their hands and feet while looking at the road. Ricky is freaking me out because he keeps looking all around him – at the wheel, out the windscreen, down at the floorboard. This is not textbook.

Ricky's about a third of the way to the bend when he decides to try the accelerator. The Ford lurches forward suddenly and then gradually slows again. Shit – easy Ricky, my mind screams. This is not good. His go at the accelerator has shot him most of the way to the bend and now he's slowly making the turn and then I'm looking at the rear of the car – he's made it around the corner. He's staying off the accelerator with only two more houses to go.

And then Ricky does something odd. Instead of turning into Sally's driveway, he brings the car to a stop in the road directly in front of the driveway. He must have his foot on the break. He cranes his neck around and he's looking over at me, with his hands raised. The expression on his face seems to say "what the hell do I do now?" I look up at Sally's house and don't see any sign of life. He could reverse the car and then drive into the driveway, but I decide the best thing to do is to call it off. Ricky can just carry on down the road, and I'll find a way of getting down the street unseen and meeting up with him. So I motion to Ricky with my hands to continue on, and a moment later he turns around and puts his hands back on the wheel. About 30 seconds elapse, and I am completely dumbstruck by what happens next.

Ricky turns the wheels hard to the left, releases the break, and rolls in a slow arc around the mailbox and across the middle of Sally's lawn. He misses a sprinkler by about a foot and finally comes to a stop in the driveway, but at the sort of angle you can only achieve if you have missed the driveway and driven over the lawn!

Oh God – this can't be happening.

There's a strong glare coming off the car windows and no matter how I jog up and down behind the hedge I simply can't make Ricky out. At least a minute passes and there's no movement anywhere – no one comes out of the house and I can't imagine what Ricky's doing in the car.

Come on Ricky, do something. Either deliver the stinking flowers or get the hell out of there – nobody drives over someone's lawn, pulls into their driveway, and then spends the rest of the afternoon there.

And then the car door opens and I can hear the 'ping ping ping' against the soft murmur of the car engine. Ricky emerges into intense sunlight with the flowers and only briefly glances over in my direction.

Good man – no use in us trying to sort things out now.

When he reaches the door and rings the bell, I start to relax slightly. For a moment, I imagine it could still be alright. Okay, the car's at a peculiar angle and I can make out faint tire marks across the grass, but nobody's come out of the house so I'll bet they didn't see Ricky's excursion across the lawn.

The door opens silently and standing in the entranceway is the large form of Sally's dad with what must be Sally's little brother hanging off one leg. I can't hear what Ricky's saying, but Sally's dad disappears into the darkness of the house.

Suddenly Sally's there and Ricky's talking but I can't make it out. And then her expression changes from bemusement to delight and I can clearly hear her say, "Oh thank you – that's so nice." Sally takes the flowers, Ricky mumbles something and then he's on his way back to the car, not even bothering to look over at me.

What a pro – my God, this could actually work.

Ricky climbs into the car and closes the door. Sally has closed the screen door but the front door is still open. I can't see Sally but she could be just inside the entranceway. I scan the house windows for any sign of an audience, but the glare blocks everything. Suddenly I'm aware of how quiet the neighborhood has become. The guy cutting his lawn is refilling the tank with gas and the boys playing basketball at the far end of the street are taking a break, sitting on the grass. The neighborhood seems enveloped in still, sun-drenched air.

Come on Ricky – put the car in reverse and wheel it out of there. We did cover reverse.

And then I hear a subtle 'click' and the tone of the engine lifts slightly. Ricky's shifted into reverse, but the car only jerks slightly and then stops. He must be turning the steering wheel hard to the left because the wheels are swinging around. I feel this intense alertness and I can't distinguish the delicate buzz of unseen insects from the low hum of mom's engine.

Suddenly the engine guns, the car shoots backwards and slams into their aluminum mailbox. There's a sickening crash of metal on pavement and the whole of the mailbox disappears under the Ford before Ricky hits the break hard and jerks to a stop.

Oh Jesus.

The back half of the car is in the street and I can see Ricky through the window again. He's frantically looking around this way and that, trying to understand what's happened, but he has no idea because the mailbox bent at the base of the pole and is lodged under the middle of the car. I am completely helpless, frozen solid to the hedge I'm clinging to. Amazingly, no one is emerging from the house yet.

And then, the car lurches forward and there's another violent screech of metal as the mail box spins out of the back of the car, coming to rest in the middle of the driveway. The car screeches to a stop. A moment later the screen door of the house swings outward and I can see Sally's dad, his expression a mixture of confusion, disbelief, and anger. Suddenly the car door flies open. Sally's dad is jogging down the driveway when Ricky jumps from the car and runs across the lawn straight towards me. I can see the sunlight flash off the car keys Ricky's grasping in his right hand and I hear Sally's dad shout, "hey you – hey." I duck down behind the hedge.

Looking at my hands I can see that I've been gripping the hedge so hard that I've cut myself, and blood is running down my right palm. I expect Ricky to emerge around the corner of the hedge any second, but instead I hear the slapping sound of his sneakers on the street growing fainter and then disappearing altogether. I hear voices and when I finally peek carefully over the hedge, I feel my heart sink. Sally's dad is standing in the road, hands on his hips, staring in the direction Ricky must have run – worse still, Sally, her mom, and little brother are standing on the driveway, staring down at the mangled mess of aluminum as if they are surveying a corpse.

Oh my God, I let a 15-year-old drive a car. They wouldn't put me in jail for that, would they? Maybe there's just a big fine or community service or maybe I have to take a course or something. Shit. What the hell do I do now? There has to be a way out of this. For a few minutes my mind is a racing mess, but eventually thoughts coalesce into something like a plan. I head for home, making sure I exit their neighborhood without being seen.

I creep through the front door of our house and into the living room. Ricky is sitting next to our little sister on the couch. The two of them are calmly eating huge bowls of peppermint chocolate chip ice-cream and watching a re-run of Bonanza. Both seem to be in a trance-like state. This is impossible. The most terrible, unimaginable thing happened less than fifteen minutes ago and Ricky is sitting on the couch eating ice cream and watching TV.

"Ricky" I whisper, "where's mom and dad?" Ricky's head shoots up, and I can tell he's startled by the sound of my voice.

"I dunno."

His eyes are wide and his voice cracks – I can tell he's really shaken.

"Come here for a minute," I hiss, motioning him into the kitchen.

My sister gives us a weird look as Ricky follows me in and we sit down at the table.

"What the hell happened?" I ask.

"I'm really sorry... I tried to do it right but there was so much to remember." He looks really upset, on the verge of tears.

"Ricky, it's not your fault. I shouldn't have let you drive. It was just stupid."

"Is mom and dad gonna find out?"

"Not if I can help it. I need the car keys."

"What are you gonna do?"

"I'm gonna go back there and see if I can get the car. If I'm quick maybe I can get the car out of there without being seen." Ricky nods and pulls the keys out of his pocket.

I approach Sally's the same route I left to make sure her family has no chance of spotting me. As I settle into my spot under the tree and behind the hedge, I can make out muted voices, but there's a male voice which seems unfamiliar. Breathing hard, I slowly let my eyes drift to the top of the hedge.

A sensation of sickness comes over me in a wave which I can feel through my throat and down my chest and stomach – my legs go weak. Out on the road is a patrol car and standing next to our car is a cop speaking to Sally's dad and mom. Sally and her little brother sit on the front step watching as the cop writes in a small black notepad. I notice that the roses, now unwrapped, are resting on Sally's lap. She holds onto her brother's hand and wraps her other hand around the roses, and I wish I could tell what she was thinking from the expression on her face, but I'm just not sure.

I can feel my heart thumping heavily, but it's slowing down slightly and so is my breathing. I know what I need to do. It's strange, but I'm feeling calmer in a way I wouldn't expect – the calmness of resignation, maybe. I'm still scared of what's going to happen, but everything is slowing down. I don't know why, but that whole business of vaginismus that Ricky was talking about suddenly comes into my mind. I take a big breath, exhale, step out of the shade and into the harsh sunlight, and head for Sally's driveway.

Advice from the Dead

When you work as an assistant in a hospital morgue for 12 years, you learn a lot about how people view the living and the dead. Death, it seems, wants to hide. I'm not suggesting that anyone makes a conscious effort to ignore us, but I can tell you that the mortuary staff are generally *unseen* or *unrecognized*. For example, when you drive onto the hospital grounds the first thing you see is the Emergency Department, a department closely associated with life and the need to save it. The next thing you notice is the maternity ward, which is of course involved in bringing new life into this world. There are signs all over the hospital which direct you to every department involved in the business of producing, saving, and repairing *life*. But you can drive right through the hospital grounds and not find the mortuary. This is because our department has been stuffed into the basement of the hospital, an area we share with the laundry division, the waste disposal department, and the pathology specimen lab (which, by the way, stinks of some unnamable mix of chemicals). Typically, people who need to visit us end up at Reception, whispering something like, *um... excuse me, can you tell me how to get to the morgue?* Like I said – unseen or unrecognized.

There's a knock on my office door and then James comes through. James works at the front desk.

"Hi ya," he says. "Your 11:00 AM visitor is here – a Mrs. Susan Bartlet."

"Thanks James," I say, rubbing my eyes. Part of my job involves escorting family members when they view one of the deceased. I check my watch and am relieved to notice that I've got five minutes before I need to take Mrs. Bartlet back to the freezer room.

"How are you doing this morning?" James asks.

I try to smile, but it takes some effort. "Okay, I guess."

"If you need me to help out today, I can," he says.

James gives me a smile and heads back to the front desk. I told James about what my husband David did. You don't imagine that your husband is going to have an affair after 19 years of marriage, and I get these periods where I feel so angry. Maybe I should have seen it coming, but I honestly didn't. I suppose David's dick hadn't been working too well for a few years, and I found Viagra in his sock drawer once. Some nights he couldn't manage it at all and then other times he was a bit soft or the thing would go off in about 3 seconds, but after all those years and three kids, it just didn't matter to me as much as it used to. We never talked about it, and maybe we should have. It's possible it bothered him more than I knew. Then came the motorcycle. David started riding around on this enormous and noisy motorcycle, which is maybe what men do when their dicks don't work so well anymore. He was more stereotype than human being for a while, and I guess it was as funny as it was annoying. He had all the gear – the jacket, the boots, even this stupid swagger we all ignored when he'd get off the thing. And then he hit that tree, wrecked the bike, broke his leg, and that was the end of motorcycling. He was such a grumpy guy, but I just thought he was cracking up in the normal and harmless way that I saw happening with some of our friends.

I rub my eyes and force myself to focus on my 11:00 AM appointment. Mrs. Susan Bartlet is here to view Mr. Tony Bartlet, a man who died yesterday afternoon on the Emergency Department from a heart attack. There's a list of family members which I look over. Susan Bartlet is probably the wife of the deceased, but you have to check because she could be a sister, a

30

mother, an aunt even. No – the file indicates that Susan Bartlet is the wife of the deceased. I rub my eyes and take a long sip of coffee.

I found out about David's affair a month ago, and of all the people it had to be Cynthia. David and I played euchre once a month with Cynthia and her husband, the sedate and unimaginative Fred. I'd always thought of Cynthia as *a woman on the cusp* – you know, a woman well past the firm and confident sexuality of younger women and yet just managing to fend off the obvious signs of old age. And my god was Cynthia putting up a fight – dyed platinum blond hair baked into a crisp presentation, gold jewelry clinking, too much expensive perfume, ridiculous high-heels. But as we sat there playing euchre month after month, it was her boobs that played the leading role. Cynthia's tops were inevitable low cut, and she'd spent so much time baking these sizable bags of fatty tissue under a sunlamp that you could make out parallel lines of cellulite running down them. I have small boobs, boobs which no doubt go unseen or unrecognized, and when I'm having a particularly *bad self-esteem day*, I feel certain that it was Cynthia's dexterous utters which led to so much of this trouble. There was a pattern which had developed. A few times over the course of an evening David would make some barely passable joke, Cynthia would laugh like some histrionic hyena with a broom stuck up its ass, Fred would work hard to suppress his irritation that card-play was being interrupted, and I would just watch the whole production in a state of mild incredulity. If that's some sort of sign that an affair is about to occur, I guess I missed it.

David told me about it, said it only happened once, and that he was very sorry. He was really upset when he told me, but I have to look at him every day now and all I can see is what he did.

I check my watch – 11:04 AM. "Come on," I say out loud and push myself up from the chair. On the way to the waiting room, I notice James waving me over.

"You taking Mrs. Bartlet through now?" he asks.

"Yeah," I say.

James points at Mrs. Bartlet through the glass window which separates our reception area from the waiting room. "She doesn't look so hot," he says. "Seems agitated, sort of panicky."

I gaze through the pane glass and look Susan Bartlet over. Her knee is pumping frenetically up and down and she's holding a tissue to her mouth and staring fixedly at the carpet.

"I wonder why she's here on her own?" I say.

"Has she got family?" he asks.

"Oh yeah," I say, thinking of the list of siblings, children, and in-laws indicated in the file.

James shrugs. "Got your tissues?" he asks.

I pat the side pocket of my uniform. "Oh yeah."

Susan Bartlet seems startled when I say her name from the door of the waiting room. "Yes, oh yes," she replies, staring wide-eyed at me.

"My name is Margaret," I say. "I'll be showing you to Mr. Bartlet."

She nods and jumps up from her seat. I lead Susan into the freezer room. The freezer room sounds cold, but the room itself isn't. Along the far wall are 20 sliding freezer units in which the bodies of the deceased are placed, and it's those units which operate at -85 centigrade. I check Mr. Bartlet's file to make sure I've got the number of the unit correct. A couple of times I've opened the wrong unit, and that's not a nice experience for family members. I place my hand on the handle of number 6 and look Susan in the eyes.

"Mrs. Bartlet, in a moment I'll open the drawer so you can view your husband. You should be aware that Mr. Bartlet's clothes have been removed, though there is a covering over his private parts. His skin will appear quite pale." It might seem silly to mention this, but you'd be surprised at how many family members expect a fully clothed loved-one, still glowing with pinkish health. Grief doesn't tend to make people very rational, and I was once even accused of stealing clothes and a ring. My little speech can help lessen the shock.

Susan nods and lowers her gaze, and I find myself looking at her. She must be in her forties. At first glance she seems attractive, and I suppose she is, in a way. But looking closely I notice a lot of make-up which covers wrinkles around her eyes and mouth, and hair which has been heavily dyed in that shade of deep red which seems so popular among young women. I slide the drawer all the way out and glance at Mr. Bartlet. He's pudgy, somewhat older than I expected, but aside from that he's like every other corpse – gray and inert, with a slight frosting of ice crystals clinging to his eyebrows. I gaze at Susan Bartlet. The tissue is held to her mouth again, her eyes are glistening saucers, and she just stands there, rigid. I simply wait because there's very little you can do at such a moment. Finally, her face collapses into an expression of anguish and a protracted sob seems to be wrenched from within her. And then she looks away and is sliding down, her back against the wall. By the time I walk around the drawer I find her lying on the floor, on her side, and she is wailing. I've seen some grief-stricken reactions in my time, but this one is pretty high up on the list. I bend down on one knee and put a hand on her shoulder.

"Mrs. Bartlet, I'm here. I'm sorry Mrs. Bartlet – it's very difficult for you to see this."

The words themselves are of course completely meaningless, but the fact that another human being is saying something can help a little. She continues to wail loudly and begins to bump her head against the marble floor. Oh shit, this is not good, and I'm not really feeling up to it either.

"Mrs. Bartlet," I say somewhat sharper, "I'm here and I want to help. Can I help you up?" The wailing continues and she is now shaking. Tears are streaming and her make-up is already a mess. I know from experience that James won't be able to hear this from the front desk and I consider leaving Susan and asking him for help, but she's bumping her head somewhat harder, which is worrying. I place my hand under her head and when she bangs it again my hand hurts a bit, which makes me a little angry. I pull my hand back and recall the file. I'm not sure what to do, but even if I can get help from James, she can't go home alone in this state.

"Mrs. Bartlet, you need your family now... I'm going to give them a call so they can help." She continues to wail and she's begun slapping the floor with her hand. I make a decision and walk quickly for the exit. As I place my hand on the door I hear her shout, "No!"

I turn to look at her and she is staring at me with an expression which is as much frightened as it is anguished. She drops her head to the ground and begins to sob painfully. I take a few steps closer.

"Mrs. Bartlet, this has been a real shock for you. You need your family for support. You shouldn't go home alone like this." She closes her eyes and the sobbing continues. I turn and walk for the exit. I'm really not feeling up to dealing with this on my own. Again, I hear Mrs. Bartlet's voice.

"No... you can't... you don't understand."

I turn and look at her, perplexed.

She continues to sob, and with some difficulty pushes herself up and sits against the wall. She puts her face into her hands. "I'm not Susan Bartlet," she says.

I find myself staring at her, stunned. What's going on? I think about the file I read and try to recall the names of family members. Have I made some mistake? No, I'm sure I haven't. Mrs. Susan Bartlet is the wife of the deceased, Mr. Tony Bartlet, and this woman told us she is Susan Bartlet. She continues to sob into her hands and I move a little closer. And then I think to myself – only family members are allowed to view the deceased. Who is this woman? And then *I've got it*. I think I know just who she is, or more to the point, *what* she is.

I kneel down next to her and look at her face through her hands and a mess of dyed hair and wrecked make-up. "Excuse me," I say, surprised at the stoniness in my tone. "If you're not Mrs. Susan Bartlet – who are you?"

The volume of her sobbing increases and she buries herself further into her hands. Her grief is genuine, that's clear enough, but I'm not falling for this tearful crap. I know too much about feminine tears. "Excuse me, I need to ask who you are," I repeat. She shakes her head and continues to sob.

I stand up, feeling suddenly light-headed... and exhausted. I haven't been sleeping well these last few weeks, and this drama at my feet has really taken it out of me. "Well..." I say, not really knowing what I'm going to say next. She looks up at me.

"My name is Cathy Willis," she says between sobs.

"Can I ask why you are here," I say. I'm pretty damn sure I know the answer, but for some reason I want to hear *her* say it.

She takes a deep breath and blows it out, involuntary sobs still coming in waves. "I'm sorry," she says. "I shouldn't have come, but I needed to see Tony. I just needed to be sure."

It's a nice effort, but she's not really telling me what I want to hear. "Can I ask, Ms. Willis, what your relationship to Mr. Bartlet was?"

"Tony and I were friends..." she says, her voice a whisper. She looks away from me, perhaps because she notices the skepticism on my face. She takes another large breath of air and releases it, painfully. "We were more than friends," she continues. "I'm sorry I lied about who I was, but they said only family could visit. I just needed to see Tony – do you understand?" The sobbing begins again. "I really loved Tony... I really did... I just can't believe he's gone."

When you do this job for as many years as I have, you develop a knack for responding therapeutically to distress. I might place a caring hand on a shoulder and say, *I can see how much he meant to you – this must be a terrible shock.* Supportive, normalizing, empathic... the cornerstones of good mortuary practice. But as I gaze at this quivering, tear-stained, and grief-stricken woman, I'm pretty sure that's *not* gonna happen.

"Why did you do it?" I hear myself say. The look of confusion on her face is almost comical.

"What?" she asks.

"I was wondering why you did it?" I ask.

"I don't understand," she says, shaking her head.

I sigh, conscious of my obvious lack of professionalism and somehow not caring, well, not caring that much. "Why did you have an affair with a married man?"

She looks up into my eyes as if I have stabbed her in the stomach, as if I have betrayed some sort of implicit feminine contract. The sobbing begins again, but now carries a somewhat hysterical tone.

"How can you ask me that?" she spits out.

"Well, it seems like a reasonable question."

She buries her face in her hands again. "It's complicated," she moans. "I loved Tony."

"Complicated..." I say. I'm aware of the cynical edge in my voice.

I stand up and look down on her huddled, shaking figure. Suddenly, I just want her out of here. I slide the drawer closed and the late Tony Bartlet is swallowed up by a frozen and silent darkness. "Ms. Willis," I say, "I need to ask you to leave this room. You're not permitted to be here."

She doesn't seem to respond or look at me. "Ms. Willis, please..." I say. She pushes herself up off the floor and then struggles to get to her feet. She's very unsteady and I notice for the first time that she's wearing quite delicate 3 inch heels. *Nice choice of footwear*, I think. She follows me to the door and takes hold of my arm for some reason. "Just a minute," she says. She takes a hand mirror out of her purse and begins to fuss over hair with her free hand and then attends to her makeup with a powdered pad. *For Christ sake.*

She replaces the mirror and pad in her purse and looks at me. "Am I in trouble?" she asks.

I think her question over carefully, and finally offer her a faint smile. "I need to complete some paperwork and get your signature," I say. "We need a signature from all our visitors." She looks uneasy and wary, but that's not my problem. "If you take a seat in the waiting room," I tell her, "I'll only be a few minutes."

James looks up at me as I enter the main office. "Everything go okay?" he asks. I point through the glass at Cathy Willis, who is staring fixedly at the carpet. "That," I say, "is not Mrs. Susan Bartlet."

An expression of confusion crosses James' face. "It's not? Then who is she?"

"Just some woman who's been fucking Mr. Bartlet," I say.

James laughs and looks astonished at my comment. "Okaaaaay..." he says. I don't swear much, so he's probably quite surprised.

"I need to make a phone call," I say. Can you keep an eye on her?"

"Sure," he says.

Back in my office, I pick up the phone and dial.

"Hello, this is Security," a male voice says.

"Hello Security, this is Margaret Thompson down in Mortuary. We've just had a visitor who claimed to be Mrs. Susan Bartlet, the wife of a deceased individual we have with us. When she was viewing the body, she acknowledged that she wasn't who she claimed to be. Her real name is Cathy Willis, and she's not a family member. She's sitting in our waiting room at the moment."

"Oh, right," the voice says wearily. "I guess we need to respond to that."

"I'd say so," I reply. "It's fraudulent misrepresentation. She's entered a morgue and viewed a body. That's a criminal offense. We have to report this to the police."

"Yea, I guess your right."

"Can you do that for me?" I ask.

"Okay," the voice says. "I'll call the police and come down now."

When I finish the call, I get a visitor's form out of my desk, and walk to the front office. I stand next to James and we gaze together at Cathy Willis through the waiting room window.

"James, I really need to get away from here for a few minutes, be on my own for a bit. Security is calling the police and then coming down. Do you mind giving her the form?"

"Sure," he says. "I'll look after things."

I walk the hospital corridors in a daze, not heading anywhere in particular. At one point I find myself at the entranceway to the maternity unit, and I sit down there, probably because the other seats are empty. The doors to the unit open and a young mother holding her newborn infant walks out, her partner beside her. They look very happy about the small miracle they have pulled off together. The mother hands the infant to her partner so she can put her jacket on, and she's having some problems with the zipper. For some reason I find myself thinking about David, but for the first time in a month I am not thinking about what he did. Instead, I recall something from many years ago, a time when the children were young. He was so happy. He'd come in from work and the kids would jump all over him, and they would wrestle together on the floor of the living room in this tangled mass of joy, and no matter how busy I was with the cooking I had to stop and watch because it was just so funny. And then he would stand up in the middle of it all with the kids hanging off his arms and he'd throw them onto the couch like this enormous bear tossing cubs around and he'd come over and wrap his arms around me and kiss me and the kids would be pulling at his legs but he was just focused on me for that moment and he'd squeeze me tight and whisper *love you babe* into my ear and then he'd let the kids drag him off to the living room and it would start all over again.

"David," I whisper. "When did you stop *seeing me*?" And I realize that the problem isn't all about Cynthia and her silly overgrown boobs. The problem had started long before that.

The young mother has sorted out her jacket and her partner hands the infant back to her. As she places the child against her chest, a loud belch comes from the infant and they burst into laughter. I watch them exit the unit, still laughing. The memory of David wrestling with the kids starts playing in my head again, and I recall how strong and handsome and confident he'd been. But he's still strong and handsome, just older and grayer and a bit softer. And then something else just *hits me*. When did David start to become so unhappy? It was something which I had hardly noticed, a creeping and insidious change. I am staring at the carpet, seeing these images of David playing with the kids, everyone shouting and laughing. And I realize that David's unhappiness was something we never really talked about, something he couldn't explain to me, and maybe something I just didn't want to look at. *Something I didn't see.*

I sigh heavily and put my face in my hands, and notice that my cheeks are wet with tears. I realize quite suddenly that I'm not angry anymore – all that is washed away and what's left is this exhaustion... and sadness. But there's something else – I'm not quite sure what I will say, but I know that I want to talk to David.

The Sadness of Battleships

I suppose everybody does something they're not proud of. Maybe they even feel ashamed and wonder if their some sort of deviant. I *do* feel bad about what I did, though to be honest, at the time I felt something like an abstracted curiosity. It's probably the sort of thing you should keep to yourself. Anyway, I need you to be patient, because there's some important context.

About two weeks ago I was wandering aimlessly along Main Street – tired, morose, resentful, though with no particular justification. I went into a couple of thrift stores because apparently I can still feel some enthusiasm for books. At one point I pulled a hard-backed book from the shelves entitled *The World's Most Evil Dictators*. The book was heavy and in good shape, and on the cover there were photos of Hitler, Mao, Stalin, Idi Amin, Saddam Hussain, and some guy I didn't recognize but later discovered was Nicolae Ceausescu. I checked the inside cover and winced at the cost – $6.00. That's a lot for a thrift store, but I guess you're not supposed to complain when they gouge you at a thrift store, what with it going for charity. I wanted the book because I was interested in the psychology of evil, or so I told myself. Of course maybe it's just one of those dopey things guys my age – I'm 35 – get interested in.

The old woman behind the counter shook uncontrollably when she accepted my money, though she worked hard to smile through it all, which came off as sort of macabre. Maybe she had that Parkinson's disease like Mohammed Ali, I don't know, but you had to hand it to her because I'll bet there's a lot of people in better shape than her and they're probably sitting on their ass at home getting stoned and feeling pretty good about how they're screwing with the system. Who knows why people get these diseases? She probably didn't even get punched in the head a few thousand times.

Did I want a plastic shopping bag? she asked, her head jerking about. She was so tiny, her skeletal arms covered in age spots and these bluish veins popping out. I found myself wondering what would happen at her funeral but then decided that was none of my business, and why was I even thinking about that?

I said 'no' to the shopping bag, but then imagined myself wandering down Main Street with a book entitled *The World's Most Evil Dictators*, and changed my mind. Ever since those high school nuts shot everyone up at Columbine, no one is above suspicion. And then there's Fred and Rosemary West and that screw-ball in Scotland who shot up a school for himself. So I changed my mind about the shopping bag. The old woman had the book in one hand and the plastic bag in the other and she was trying to put the book into the bag, but her arms were flying about like some strange bird trying to take off and she kept missing, and I didn't know if I was meant to help or if that was going to make things worse. I looked around the shop and realized she was there on her own, and I felt a little mad they left her like that. So I said, "can I help you with that," and the old woman said, in this tiny voice you could barely hear, "oh, yes dear."

I dropped the book on the floor near the desk in my office when I got home. I don't know why I didn't take the time to put it in my book case. Maybe it's because I'm depressed as shit and depressed people drop books (and socks, and groceries, and pretty much anything) on the floor. Maybe I didn't know where in my bookcase to place it. I don't really have an *Evil Dictator Section*, or something like that. So the book just lay on the floor for two weeks and I probably glanced at it more than once when I went in and out of my office, wondering why I don't put it away.

This evening I had my daily jerk-off session, which I suppose is what I've been trying to tell you about all along. It had been a normal enough day – people at work hassling me and I'm trying to smile at them because it's my job, which, come to think of it, is probably how that Parkinson's lady feels. I work in a cell phone shop on the high street and I've got these targets about how many phones I'm meant to sell. I've worked there for 3 years, which is sad, because for one thing my work-colleagues look about 14 years old, and for another thing, I've never once met my sales target. I don't know why they don't fire me. The problem is, all day I get these customers coming in and telling me their phones don't work. They get real agitated and sometimes aggressive if they're middle-aged or they're just apologetic and befuddled if they're older. The phones always work of course, but I spend ages helping customers set up their accounts properly, adjusting their settings, and mostly just teaching them how to use the damn thing. My manager said, *hey, if they can't figure out how to work their phones, that's not our problem.* But cell phones are more complicated than you think. Plus, I don't manage to sell many phones because, irony upon irony, I don't even like the things. I got one which sits on my bureau at home. When it was new I suppose I got excited like most people about the wiz-bang technology and I sent a few text messages to the kids at work and this one guy who is meant to be a friend, but no one texted me back. Technology – what a thing. Did Henry David Thoreau say something like, *what if we do finally manage to lay down that trans-Atlantic cable, and the first thing we hear is that the queen is wearing a new hat?* I prefer the self-enclosing assurance of books. Whatever.

Anyways, about the jerk-off. I get home from work at 5:30 PM and my wife is mad at me because I forgot to pick up milk and our two boys are shouting and pulling at me and then I'm down on the floor playing marbles and doing this puzzle which is too complicated for them and all the while I'm trying to keep these little sadistic animals from killing each other, and right in the middle of it I spill a whole glass of beer on the carpet and my wife gets the wrong end of the stick and shouts at our youngest one and he starts howling and I have to explain that I spilled the beer and my wife is so pissed-off she won't even look at me, and I feel so god-damned stiff in the legs from playing down there on the floor for 2 hours... well, probably a lot of guys are gonna need a jerk-off, which, as I said, is pretty much a normal day.

At bedtime, the boys come up with a long list of absurd stalling tactics, and you'd have to appreciate the sheer ingenuity of their performance if it weren't so damn annoying. I finally get them into bed, and maybe they feel a little guilty about what bastards they've been all evening because they become rather sweet for about ten seconds just before dropping off.

I climb the stairs to the top floor, second pint in hand (not counting the one that spilled), and head for my box-room office and computer. I pause outside the bedroom because I can hear my wife changing her cloths. No doubt she's getting ready to go out with her girlfriends. Three or four nights a week she goes out, dancing at clubs or maybe to some bar. She never once asked me to go with her, but I would probably hate it anyway. I'm not much of a dancer and I don't really like a lot of noise.

The thing is, I want to go in the bedroom, but I hesitate because I'm pretty sure she doesn't want me in there when she's getting changed. It's stupid, if you think about it. She's sort of comfortable with her body, like she will wear a bikini or short skirts in the summer. But if her own husband just happens to wander into his own bedroom and she happens to be getting changed, well apparently that's not okay.

I push open the door and enter the room, and she glances at me. She pulls a dress over her head hurriedly, and starts buttoning it up. She's already got her make-up on.

"I'm going out tonight… I'm late."

I feel like saying, *I know, you go out most nights, don't you?* But I don't say anything. I look at the rug mostly, but sneak a few glances at her. The light from the hallway illuminates her muscular legs, and she looks great. I want to touch her, but what I really want is for her to *stop* and come over and put her arms around me, to feel me.

She looks up and places her hands on her hips. "You okay?" she says, but there's an edge of impatience in her tone, and I know she just wants to get the hell out of the house, meet up with her friends, smoke some pot, and let off steam. She's probably had a few hassles herself today.

"Yea, I'm okay," I say.

I go into my office and turn the computer on. Jerking-off involves a little routine I go through. Probably most people have some routine, even women I'll bet. Routines are no doubt useful because you can *trust* in them to work. That's got to be the point of a routine. I've got a role of toilet paper I keep in my desk drawer. While the computer is warming up, I always get a wad of toilet paper which I put on my desk. Next, apply some petroleum jelly. You see what I mean by a routine?

The internet porn I look at is the free stuff and it's probably normal enough. Of course I'm not sure what's normal anymore. I suppose it's possible that *sick* is the new normal. It's not as if you can join a focus group to understand that sort of thing. So I'm doing my thing and drinking beer as successive pages download, and everything is happening just as it's meant to, which means that I feel good, *really* good. More than that, I feel powerful, forceful, and there's something quite intoxicating about all this masculine potency. I am captain of my ship, commander and chief, a ruler of sorts. And as my authority over these unsuspecting fleshy subjects approaches its high point, I stand up and reach for the wad of toilet paper... only to discover that tonight I have forgotten to get it ready. Realizing that I am past the point of no return, and not wanting to jizz on my keyboard, I quickly turn to the left and spurt an off-white blob into the air...

As the last convulsions wind down I stand there dumbstruck, gazing at the strange accident on the floor. My blob of semen has landed squarely across the front cover of *The World's Most Evil Dictators*. I managed to hit Stalin, Mao, and a small bit of that Ceausescu guy. Hitler, Saddam Hussain, and Idi Amin escape, but that's not the point. The point is... what is the point? I wipe myself off and sit down. I feel terrible, but stare at the book with, as I said, an abstracted curiosity. There's something awful and yet important about what I've done, and I feel the need to laugh out loud and turn myself into the authorities all at once. Instead, I just sit and stare sadly for a while, wondering what's wrong with me. My wife will have left a while ago, by now. Finally, I wipe the book clean with a damp washcloth, place the damn thing in my book-case, and take a shower.

Not knowing what else to do, I go down stairs, make some tea, and end up watching this documentary on the History Channel about the sinking of the battleship Bismarck. Those images of that big battleship and everything that happened materialize before my eyes like some odd dream you probably just keep to yourself the next morning.

The following day the world and my routine in it appears before me, familiar, and yet strange in its familiarity. I deal with the usual stream of confused customers until about 1 PM, and then walk down Main Street with my lunch bag. I eat on my own at this small park which is wedged between a decaying church and some forgotten brick buildings. On the way I pass the charity shop I bought *The World's Most Evil Dictators* at, and stand at the window, staring inside, like a criminal compelled to return to the scene of his crime. The tiny Parkinson's lady is there, on her own, and she's got a small line of customers to deal with. I watch her as she tries to get some videos into a carrier bag, smiling in that embarrassed way, her arms shaking and flying about. Why the fuck don't they give her some help? I wonder again.

I sit on a bench in the park and munch absent-mindedly on a peanut butter and jam sandwich my wife made this morning. Two walking paths meet right in the middle of the park, and just where the paths cross there's this religious nut. Everyday he stands there, smiling serenely at each passerby, and next to him is this 6 foot, hand-painted sign which reads GOD IS YOUR SAVIOUR – REPENT TODAY AND ACCEPT HIS DIVINE LOVE. I just think, *man, that guy must have done something really bad.* The park is filled with people, some sitting on benches, others just walking through, and they all look very normal – normal attire, normal enough conversations, normal behavior. Of course I probably look quite normal too, so who can really say?

The usual circus of events play themselves out this evening, except I manage not to spill my beer. I endure the familiar hassles of getting the boys off to sleep and stand outside my bedroom for a minute or two, listening to my wife getting dressed for the evening. I go upstairs to my office, turn on my computer and glance over at the *World's Most Evil Dictators* in my bookcase. I think about the toilet paper and petroleum jelly, and realize that I just haven't got it in me tonight. But the computer's on now, so I check my emails. I've got three pieces of spam – Rolex watches, Viagra, and some bank in Nigeria that's got a great investment opportunity for me. I turn the computer off.

I can hear my wife still getting dressed through the bedroom door. I should probably just leave her alone, but I push open the door and sit on the bed, looking down at the carpet. She's wearing a dress I haven't seen before, and it looks great on her. I love the curve of her waist as it makes its way over her hip and down her leg. I love the way her skin smells. I guess I just love her.

"I'm so late," she says, doing several buttons up hurriedly.

I nod in acknowledgement. There's this numbness I've been feeling lately, or maybe for a long time, it's hard to tell. But something's giving way and I can't stop it. I can feel two big tears run down both cheeks, hot and silent, and my stomach muscles pull into knotted rhythmic spasms as I try to keep control. My shoulders and arms begin to shake with whatever this emotion is. I look straight at the floor, but I can feel her close now. She's on her knees in front of me, her warm hand on the side of my neck.

"Oh God, are you okay?" she says.

I am gulping for air, my chest heaving, and my shoulders and arms continue to shake.

"No," I say. "I don't think I am."

She works herself closer to me, wraps her arms around me and buries her head in my neck. We seem to rock together slightly. She's moving her hand up and down my back, and I don't know if there's a name for what I'm feeling. I think we stay like that for some time.

I'm not that bothered about what happened in my office any more, you know, that thing that involved Stalin, Mao, and a bit of that Ceausescu guy, and maybe I'm feeling somewhat lighter these days. But for some reason, I do find myself thinking of that documentary I watched about the sinking of the Bismarck. The whole thing just seems so sad. Here was this enormous and incredibly powerful battleship – 823 feet in length, 15-inch guns and 13-inch metal armor plating. Yeah, I looked it up. And yet a single antiquated British biplane stuck one tiny torpedo into the hull, and that was the end. It's just really sad, if you think about it.

Digging a Hole

For as far back as I can remember, I have always been able to make music in my head. When I was a kid, it was so easy, so natural. It wasn't even *making* music, like it was a job. Music just happened. Let's say my family was out for one of our Sunday drives – for no particular reason, I would begin to feel a nice rhythm. That rhythm wasn't the music yet, but it would begin in my right leg, which would start pumping with the heel of my foot going up and down. I would let my head bob slightly with the leg pulse, and then the music would start. I heard the music in my head, but strange as it seems, I could use different parts of my mouth to represent different *sounds* or *instruments*. My teeth would knock lightly together, my tongue would make a silent movement against the roof of my mouth, and the main melody was always produced by humming. Sometimes the music I heard in my head even became too complicated for my mouth to keep up with, and I'd have to use my toes to play new voices or rhythms.

But that was when I was a kid. That was when it was always easy and fun. I'm 23 years old, and just now I'm staring down at 88 black and white keys, trying to remember the progression of chords I was playing just 2 minutes ago. The song I'm working on is okay, but I worry that it's too much like the last song I wrote. I try the series of chords again and sing nonsense words to them, trying to find the right lyric melody. I get the chord progression wrong again, and curse myself.

When I *played* the music in my body as a kid I could usually keep the whole works fairly quiet, but there were times when my mother would hear the humming, which was the loudest part, and tell me in an angry tone to *stop making that noise.* Looking back on events, I imagine mom had read something about psychotic or autistic children in Reader's Digest and was afraid I would turn out to have a mental illness. I never told anyone how music was for me. I was just a kid, and I was entertaining myself, like kids do.

My dad sticks his head into the room and scowls at me, shaking his head, and then goes out the front door. I've heard his speech enough times that now he just needs to scowl. *You've got a university degree collecting dust and 25,000 in school loans to pay to the bank and you just have no idea what to do with your life. I didn't go to college, you know. When I was your age, I was married and had four kids. And I worked my tail off...60...80 hours a week. Let me guess, you don't know who you are and all that stuff, right? Hey man, are you searching for yourself?* When dad asks these questions, he's apparently trying to mimic what he thinks is a liberal, hippie dialect. It isn't a bad impression considering that he missed the whole movement on account of Catholic morality, political conservatism, the four kids, and the 60 to 80-hour workweek. Every time I hear that speech of his I feel... immobilized. I don't blame him, though. I think about my crummy resume and a couple of interviews I probably blew on account of not wanting the jobs. I wonder if I'm irresponsible and lazy. Sometimes I think about people I graduated with and what they're doing.

I try the chord progression again, get it wrong again, and then decide I'm probably annoying dad because I'm playing the same music over and over. Dad's just outside the window now, working in the garden, and I can't bear the weight of his silent disapproval so close by. I decide to take a walk.

I exit the front door and glance over at dad who's digging into the ground, pulling out some weeds. He retired last year but for some odd reason still wears the same brown slacks and leather shoes he wore to work all those years. There is something so incongruous about a chubby 65-year-old man squatting down and pulling weeds out of a garden in brown slacks, black dress socks, and leather shoes.

The day is warm and bright and there's a slight breeze. A big yellow school bus flies past, noisy with screaming kids and a grinding engine. It reminds me of the last day of school before summer vacation when you're a kid – you know, that day when you anticipate the last bell for hours and then your heart is bursting all the way home, and the day is a perfect reminder of all the beautiful days you have ahead of you. Seven-month-old brown leaves fly up in the wake of the rushing bus. It's *really* summer.

When I approach the circular turn-around at the end of the street, I see a kid with a shovel. The turn-around contains three houses and a vacant lot, which sits between the second and third house. The kid, he must be about five years old, is digging in the vacant lot. The scene looks pretty comical because the shovel is full-size and almost as long as the kid is tall. As I walk the perimeter of the turn-around, something about the kid makes me want to watch. The kid doesn't even take notice of me – he just keeps working at the tough soil, and I can hear him coming up against weeds and rocks. I somehow expect that he will wear himself out and take a break or quit, but he doesn't miss a beat. There's an intensity and concentration about him that won't allow me to continue on, so I stand back about 10 feet and watch.

Looking to my left I notice Mr. Schneider for the first time. He's lying in one of those fold-up lawn chairs and watering the already green grass with one of those garden hoses that has an attachment that sprays the water for you. He seems to be watching us.

I'm struck suddenly by the contrast between the empty lot and the Schneider's place. There's a perfectly straight line which is formed by the meeting of Mr. Schneider's trimmed green grass and the overgrown brownish, weedy property of the lot. It looks a little absurd. I scan the Schneider's house. Mr. Schneider had paid someone to put on that plastic siding with the wood grain molded right into it. He talked to dad about it once, and apparently the company who manufactures it guarantees that the stuff will not need replacing for 100 years. It occurs to me that the whole place looks like one of those scale models that some architect puts together with little pieces of balsa wood, transparent glue, and finishing paint. I mean those models covered in glass that you see in shopping malls.

Mr. Schneider is out of his lawn chair now and heading with slow, heavy paces to the hose faucet. He kills the hose and starts out toward us. When he reaches the edge of his lawn and the lot he appears to step *over* the property line as if it were a short, electrified fence.

I think he's been retired for a couple of years. Thin strands of grey hair cling to the side of his perspiration-strewn head and his face is puffy and blotchy. His nose seems bloated and you can see these tiny, reddish veins which run over it. Mr Schneider has that strange combination of comparatively thin legs and a huge gut. This guy really carries some weight above the belt, and never tucks in his shirts. The shirt he's wearing is one of those short-sleeve numbers with a Hawaiian flower pattern and there's stitched lettering on the pocket which reads *Myrtle Beach*. Powder-blue shorts appear from beneath his shirt and run down to his knees.

"Hey-ya there Peter," he calls.

"Hi Mr. Schneider," I reply.

The boy looks up for a moment, but this does not interrupt his work on the hole.

"Your dad tells me you're looking to settle into a career now that you've finished college."

"I um… yeah, I guess so," I say.

"Have you got some definite plans yet?"

"No," I say, "I'm not sure about…"

"Have you got a starting place?"

"Well, I…"

"Ya know Peter," he continues, "I have to admit, I had a conversation with your father last week and I've been meaning to talk with you about…"

Mr. Schneider's train of thought seems to get interrupted as he suddenly takes notice of the boy, whom he gazes at intently.

"Hey… hi there kid," he says.

Then he glances back at his own property as if to make absolutely sure that the kid is not actually digging into the middle of his lawn.

"I guess it's okay for you to be digging there, huh?" he says, sounding indignant.

The boy stops digging and looks up at Mr. Schneider. What feels like a long silence elapses and the boy gapes upward with an expression that looks half-confused and half-scared. I think the boy is wondering if he's done something wrong. Eventually, Mr. Schneider replies, "well, I suppose there's no reason why you can't dig in an empty lot."

Looking at me, he continues – "you never know what they'll let you do and what they won't."

"Who?" I ask..

"What?" he says, wearing an expression which probably looks as perplexed as my own.

I try to sort out the confusion. "You said, you never know what they will let you do or what they won't… who do you mean?"

"Oh," Mr Schneider replies. "You know, the people that make the rules about things."

This doesn't really make things much clearer, but I've lost interest anyhow.

He again looks at the boy, who has resumed his digging. Mr. Schneider appears a little perplexed.

"Say there son, why are you digging that hole?"

"I'm… I'm digging in the ground," the boy replies.

"I can see you're digging son, but why are you digging?"

The boy looks bewildered as Mr. Schneider waits for an answer.

"I got a shovel out of the garage. Mom said I could take it so I could use it. She said I could shovel if I wanted, but I wasn't sposed to shovel in the yard. She said I could shovel here. Mom said I had to remember to bring the shovel back. I brang the shovel and so I was shovelling."

Mr. Schneider looks a little frustrated.

"Son, I know you're shovelling. I mean… you're making a hole. That's good. Now, what's the hole for?"

The boy seems more confused than ever and a pained expression appears in his eyes and around his mouth. He looks down at the large silver blade of the shovel and the six-inch hole at his feet.

"I'm digging like this," he says.

With a grunt, the kid hefts the shovel into the hole and jumps hard and awkwardly onto the blade. I can hear the blade hit a rock, and the boy nearly falls to the ground. He looks up at us to see if his demonstration has helped to explain matters.

Mr. Schneider looks at me. His hands are on his hips now and he shows me a crooked grin that contains an odd mixture of puzzlement and disapproval.

"Kids sure are funny, aren't they? Look, anyways, I was telling you about talking with your dad the other day and there were a few things I thought I might mention. Now I know you're getting older and I don't mean to sound like I'm telling you what to do, but I've learned a few things over the years."

I can hear the boy digging again, but the sound of the shovel swooshing against weeds and chinking against rocks seems to have slowed.

"Peter, the thing is, you have to plan for the future. You've got to decide what's important. A good, steady job that you can count on is important. A good wife and a family are important. Peter, I don't mind telling you that I've worked hard for the things that I have – the house, the boat, the time-share, and I'm not saying all this to brag. I'm not a rich man, but Peter, I have something that a lot of people don't – I've got security…"

I suddenly notice a subtle change come over Mr. Schneider. He continues talking as before but seems distracted. He no longer looks into my eyes, but stares off to his right. I look over quickly and notice that a school bus has stopped in front of the house next to the Schneider's. Looking back at Mr. Schneider I can see that he is gazing at the open door of the bus. Glancing back at the bus, I can see that Susan Fulcher is stepping out, laughing and throwing back her long blond hair. I haven't seen her in a few years and I suppose she's about 15 or 16 by now. She sure has changed. Her boobs bounce slightly with every step. She wears these tight fitting bleached white pants, and the lines of her underwear can be seen clearly through them. You can even make out a pattern of red hearts which are part of the underpants material. Turning to face Schneider, I can see that he is watching Susan intently, his eyes following her movements as she must be making her way up the front porch. I have no idea what he's saying, but I notice his voice has become monotone. He works his hands beneath the Myrtle Beach shirt and squeezes them down into his pockets.

When the front door to Susan's place slams shut, it seems to jar Mr Schneider back into the conversation.

"Did you ever think of going into sales, Peter?"

"You mean like selling things to people?" I ask.

"Well yes... I mean no... I mean there's a lot to it... I'm talking about being a *Salesman*. Did you ever think about being a *Salesman*?"

"I guess I haven't thought about it."

This is not altogether true. Mr. Schneider continues to instruct me, probably about the benefits of the sales industry, but I'm distracted by a memory. About two months ago I saw an ad in the paper which read, 'SALES JOB – MAKE 1,000 DOLLARS A WEEK'. They weren't allowed to tell me about the job over the phone, but if I went to a particular office park, I would hear all about it and would receive an interview. When I arrived, I was surprised to be ushered into a room with about 30 other people. We all sat and listened to a lengthy lecture on how incredibly poisonous tap water was and how we were all going to make a mint selling water purifiers through home demonstrations. It took about an hour for the presenter to get to the part about how we were selling on 100% commission. They had some of their current sales people standing around the edges of the room, and I remember this one guy about my age that was covered in tattoos and looked like he had been up partying for the last month. I had even put on the suit and tie grandpa had bought me when I graduated. Jesus, I felt like such an idiot. I snuck out at a coffee break and didn't feel like going home, so I drove to a mall and bought a Kafka novel which made me feel like shit when I read it.

Suddenly I'm aware that Mr. Schneider's voice has stopped, and I experience a spurt of anxiety because I realise I have no idea of what he's been talking about. He stares at me and all I can do is nod stupidly. I'm relieved when Schneider turns his attention to the boy. His hands are up on his hips again.

I feel like I want to push on and this seems as good a time as any to excuse myself, so I say, "I guess I'd better be going – I'll see ya later Mr. Schneider." He says goodbye, and I begin to walk the rest of the turn-around loop. When I reach the Schneider's driveway, I hear Mrs. Schneider call out my name. I hadn't seen her at first because she had been hidden behind some bushes. She's motioning for me to come and see her. I sigh inwardly and make my way up the driveway.

"Hello Peter," she squeals.

I think I get sort of amazed when I see a really fat lady. I don't know if other people have this reaction. It's just that the whole thing is so hard to believe. Mrs. Schneider reclines on a chaise lounge and wears a shirt and long pants made of a material that I guess was designed to stretch to vast proportions. Big mounds pull in every direction, and I notice there's a paperback resting on her vast stomach. I sense that she will want to know how dreadful my life is going, so I get a jump on the conversation.

"Hi Mrs. Schneider, is the book any good?"

"Oh, this... it's nothing, really... just some pleasure reading at the moment."

The phrase *at the moment* seems to imply that she alternates her pleasure reading with books on modern physics and political philosophy. I'm guessing not.

She has a chubby finger shoved between the pages of this enormous paperback and I scan the picture on the front cover. There's a beautiful young woman with waist-length, shining blond hair. She wears a long white dress which looks like it's from the 17th century, maybe. There's a bare-chested, big muscled man with jet-black hair and olive skin standing mostly behind the woman. His eyes are closed. Her big white breasts are threatening to fall out of her bodice and drop straight into his hands, which hold her firmly, if not roughly, about the waist. He's wearing a big sword which juts down to his ankle. One of her hands grips hard at one of his wrists, but in a rather unconvincing way.

Mrs. Schneider is talking and giggling, but I find that I am attending to something else. I'm feeling an emotion which is strange because it's new to me. Suddenly there wells up into my mind an image of the digging boy and all at once I need to know what's happening in the lot. I look over my shoulder, and there's the boy, but rather than digging he's staring up at Mr. Schneider. Although Schneider has his back to me, I can tell from his gestures that he's talking to the boy. I feel compelled to know what he's saying. Mrs. Schneider looks disappointed when I excuse myself.

When I reach the lot, I can hear Mr. Schneider saying, "... now when they build a house, for example, they have to dig out the area which will become the basement. You're digging too, so why might you be digging?"

The boy stares down at the hole. He looks confused and I know that he doesn't understand what Schneider is talking about. I know that he doesn't know what to say. I know that what looks like a very tiny and worthless hole to Mr. Schneider is beginning to look like a very tiny and worthless hole to the boy. I feel for the boy in a way I can't describe, but there's a thick and painful sensation in my upper chest and throat. I'm choking back something and I want to act somehow, but I have no idea what to do.

Then, right in the middle of this monumental moment of indecision, Mr. Schneider chooses to excuse himself. This seems incredible somehow. I mean, here is a really important juncture and I'm supposed to do or say something significant, and Mr. Schneider loses interest, and with "see ya later kid... so long Peter..." he's gone. I stare open-mouthed at Mr. Schneider's departing form, struck dumb and inert. Not knowing what else to do, I look back to the boy.

The boy hardly seems to notice me and he's leaning against the shovel and staring into the hole. I still want to say something. He stares down at his hole for what seems like the longest time and... the only way I can describe it is to say that he looks... immobilized.

Suddenly, I find my words. It's hard to speak because there's this thick pain in my throat, but I hear myself saying, "you know, I like to dig with a shovel. Can I have a turn and dig with your shovel – just for a minute?"

He looks thoughtful for a moment and finally says, "okay."

I put the shovel into what looks like a softer spot and jump as hard as I can onto the blade. It jams into the earth. I jump again, throw the dirt, and then jump a third time. The whole process is amazing, really. Jumping hard, the sudden impact of my sneaker on the blade. The ground breaking. The rocks complaining. I can sense the boy moving in for a closer look when I hear him say, "why are you digging the hole?"

"I'm digging," I say, "because I like to dig. I like to jump on the shovel as hard as I can. I like to throw the dirt. I like to see how I'm making the hole in the ground."

"I like to dig too," he says. "I like to jump on the shovel and make the hole. Do you wanna watch how I can do it?"

"Sure," I say, and I hand him the shovel.

He puts the blade back into his hole and pushes at the handle so that the shovel is straight. With a big little kid leap and a grunt, he lands on the blade. He hits a rock, the handle leaps to the right, and the boy lands hard on the ground. Jumping up, he gets the shovel ready for another try. Coming down hard on the blade he says "POW." Jumping again, he yells "BAM."

I watch for a while and then say goodbye and turn to go. He dismisses me with a smile and a brief wave as he prepares another jump.

As I walk back home I feel a rush of something powerful, which is like heat, and strength, and insight which does not need to explain itself. The neighborhood sights and smells are sharp and clear. All at once I recognize with perfect conviction that everything is going to be all right. Things would be difficult – maybe even very difficult – but I know that from this moment onwards, everything is going to be okay. The neighborhood seems to move by a little quicker.

My body feels light and prickly energy beats through my chest and arms. For a moment my eyes close and my teeth clench and I smile through an expression which to others might look like pain, but it's intense pleasure, and I draw a huge breath of air into my lungs and give out a shout... and then I'm running full-out and suburbia is flying past jerkily and noiselessly... and I see in my mind an image of the piano waiting for me in the living room.

Missing Person

I'm lying in bed, thinking about how nice it would be to just go to sleep, but Cathy is down in the kitchen, shouting and slamming cupboard doors. Apparently her dinner party was a disaster. Apparently it was my fault. Molly, my Labrador, is lying on the floor next to the bed and looking at me, concern in her eyes. She knows what's going on. She's heard it all before.

I can hear Cathy coming up the stairs now, muttering and stomping. I'm facing the wall, but I can feel her presence behind me like storm clouds.

"And something else Ed," she yells. "Why did you have to bore people by telling them you work in the finance department? You work for the FBI, which actually sounds interesting. You don't have to bore everyone with the details of all the stupid paperwork you do."

I'm remembering this moment from earlier this evening where I was talking with a couple of women from Cathy's drama club. We're holding our drinks, standing there talking about I can't remember what, and Cathy comes up behind me and pats the front of my suit coat, and she says, *now don't worry girls, Ed might be FBI, but he's not packing any heat tonight.* They all laugh like demented hyenas.

"I know you're not asleep Ed," she shouts.

I might be staring at the wall opposite me, but I can see her alright, hands on her hips, eyes narrowed, all that make-up and lipstick, her mouth drawn up in a spiteful knot.

There's more coming for sure, but I keep quiet because

there's just no point. I sure do wish I could go to sleep, though.

On my way to and from the staff cafeteria, I pass the FBI's *Missing Persons Department*. You know you're outside Missing Persons because they always have about twenty 8 X 10 photos pinned up. There are actually thousands of missing persons at any one time, and you can go into the department and flip through photos of each and every one. When employees are new to the FBI, you might see them stop and look at the photos – but you get used to it, and after a while I don't think staff even notice them anymore.

That's why I was surprised when I stopped to look at a particular photo. It was a picture of a middle-aged man – about my age, I guess. He's standing in front of a cliff-edge in bright sunlight with what looks like the Grand Canyon behind him. It's a color photo, and the man wears blue jeans and a red and white checked shirt. He's white, with graying hair and a medium build. In fact, everything about him is rather medium – I mean ordinary. There's a collie sitting next to him and he smiles at whoever is taking the picture. I think the reason you *stop* looking at photos of missing persons is because after a while they all start to look the same – kids who have probably been abducted by a stranger or snatched by a parent who feels aggrieved about their custody rights, or angry adolescents who decided to run away. But you don't usually see middle-aged men who look like they're on vacation. Beneath the photo is typed:

Michael Huber
Missing since January 2nd, 2015
$1,000 reward for information leading to Michael's safe return

Missing for 10 months, I think.

That photo wasn't much more than a curiosity for me the first time I saw it. But each day I walk to lunch I find myself stopping to study it, and every time I'm left with the same perplexing thought: How can a middle-aged, middle-class man become a missing person? I even printed a copy of his Missing Person photo off the FBI's website and carry it in my pocket. I'll pull it out a few times a day and wonder about where Michael is, which I know is a strange thing to do.

I have security clearance to access FBI case files for the purpose of doing spot-check audits on expense claims that officers make. Like if an officer claims for travel or hotel expenses, then there should be a record in the file that they actually had to visit someone or that they traveled to another city. There's probably several reasons I shouldn't read Huber's file. For one thing, it's against policy to look at a file for reasons outside the remit of your job. For another, I think I've been pretty depressed lately and I'm getting behind on the R-62 expense claim forms for this month, and that means my manager will be on my case again. *Ed, I need to see you in my office. Ed, there's no excuse for not finishing a job that simple.* You get the idea.

There's no reason to hide the *M. Huber* file tag when other staff walk by, but that's just what I find myself doing. The agent attached to the case is called Bob Teamerson, and I can tell straight off that the case is *informally closed*. Officially, the case has been open for 10 months, but over the past 3 months all Bob Teamerson has done is log two calls from Mrs. Huber. Apparently, Mrs. Huber wanted to know if any new evidence of her husband's whereabouts had surfaced. It hadn't.

It looks like Bob Teamerson interviewed Mrs. Barbara Huber, Michael's work manager, and the bus driver on duty for the route Michael took on the morning of January 2nd. He also did a check on bank and credit card activity before and following Michael Huber's disappearance, and a criminal records check. It seems that Michael Huber is 48 years old, a loan officer at a local bank, married to Barbara Huber for 22 years, and has an 18-year-old daughter. According to Mrs. Huber, Michael left for work, as usual, on January 2nd. But according to the bank manager, he simply never arrived. The bus driver doesn't recall him getting on the bus that morning, but couldn't be sure. In their own words, Mrs. Huber and his manager give descriptions of Michael which are so similar, it's strange: He's a nice, quiet guy who is pleasant to others but keeps to himself. His manager said he did okay at his job, but that he wasn't very ambitious and sometimes he seemed distracted. His wife mentioned that he liked to read and didn't have too many friends. His wife and manager were *shocked* by his disappearance. Certainly, Michael didn't have any enemies, they both agreed. *I can't imagine anyone wanting to hurt him*, his manager had said. The criminal records check turned up one speeding ticket over the past 31 years, which occurred in 1988. Financial activity was fairly normal before the disappearance, and then just stopped. About three months ago the agent had written the words *no apparent evidence of criminal wrongdoing, but disappearance inconclusive*, and that's about when, I suspect, he gave up and decided focusing on other cases.

There was one other thing that was interesting. Teamerson made a note that some bum had walked in off the street and told the receptionist in Missing Persons that he knew where Huber was, but that he wanted the reward money right away. Apparently, when the receptionist explained that it didn't work that way, the bum got angry and walked out. I made lots of notes.

My daughter isn't speaking to me because I won't buy her a car. She doesn't say that's the reason why, but I know it is. I've tried to explain to her that a car, even a second-hand one, is expensive. But when I tell her about running costs, repair bills, annual inspection... she wouldn't listen. All she does now is mumble shallow responses at me whenever I try to ask her about school, or whatever. I don't know what to do about it. I tried to raise the issue this morning.

"I know you're angry at me about not getting you a car, but I simply don't have the money."

She continued staring at her Cornflakes. We're only sitting at the same table because I joined her.

"Just forget it, alright."

"Well, the fact that you won't talk to me because I won't buy you a car doesn't seem right."

Her head comes up quick, long black hair flashing. "No – the car isn't the reason I don't like talking. The reason is you're a geek. You dress and act like a geek. I have a geek for a dad."

She leapt up and made a quick exit from the kitchen. I can't recall when she started talking to me like that. I think that maybe I should have done something about it long ago, but it seems too late now.

I park my car on the road and scan the Huber's property. There isn't much to distinguish it from countless other suburban homes. I recall my phone call to Barbara Huber. I'm sure we'd never met, but her voice sounded familiar somehow.

"Hello."

"Hello, this is Ed Walker…"

I didn't want to mention the FBI, but I just couldn't see Mrs. Huber meeting with some total stranger with no links to law enforcement.

"I'm with the FBI… I was hoping to speak with you about Michael and wondering if you wouldn't mind meeting."

"Yes, that would be fine. Is there any news on Michael?"

I hadn't thought about lifting her hopes, and I felt bad about that immediately.

"There's nothing significant which is new, I'm afraid. I was hoping to speak about Michael generally."

"Oh," she'd replied. "Yes, I'd be glad to."

When I'd hung up, I was pretty sure I had just ended my career. Looking through a file is one thing, playing FBI agent is something else. Part of me found that scary, part of me was past caring.

Barbara Huber opens the door cheerfully and seems pleased to see me in a way that's surprising, but also eases my anxiety. I look her over as I follow her to the couch in the living room. She strikes me as a woman at war with time – fully entrenched in middle age, but fighting off anything resembling old age. She works hard at it too. There's a lot of makeup, but it's been put on with great care. She dresses like those somewhat younger models I've noticed in my wife's catalogs, and I can tell her clothes were designed to hide the plumpness which gathers around her tummy and bottom. She wears gold bracelets and necklaces, and her perfume is heavy with some floral scent. She doesn't ask me if I want tea – she just smiles and tells me she's going to make some tea and how did I take it?

I can hear her humming and singing to herself in the kitchen, which makes me think she's one of those people who don't like things to be too quiet. She hands me my tea and sits next to me on the couch, rather than in the chair opposite, which is surprising.

"Mrs. Huber, I do appreciate that you've taken this time to see me, but I feel I should really let you know my role and why I'm here."

"Oh yes, of course. But only if you call me Barbara."

"I do work for the FBI, but I'm in the finance department. I'm sure you have an agent already working on Michael's case, and I should let you know that I'm not involved in the case. I mean it's not my place to act like an agent, if you see what I mean."

I keep a close eye on Mrs. Huber, watching for any sign of annoyance or disappointment. But she just looks straight at me, trying to figure me out. There seems nothing to do but continue.

"In a way, I suppose it's difficult to explain why I'm here. It's just that... well, when I saw Michael Huber's photo outside of the Missing Persons Department... there was something that struck me about it. Maybe it's because he and I are almost the same age. I'm sure my visit seems strange to you. I just wanted you to know that I'm sorry for you. That I hope you find Michael."

"No, I don't think it's strange," she says. "The agent on the case – Mr. Teamerson – I think he's pretty useless."

There's a pause and I imagine I'm supposed to say something, but I don't know what. I just let the silence sit there, hoping she'll start to talk about Michael. It doesn't take long.

"We were shocked. He just went off to work one day and then he was gone. He never made it to the bank and no one has heard of him since. I can't imagine who would want to hurt Michael or what could have happened. It's just so unthinkable... " There's something dramatic in her tone and the expression on her face, the way her hands are waving about.

She's a real talker. She discusses Michael's job, the fact that he loved to read, that he liked using the computer and watching nature programs. She says that he never seemed to get upset about much. After a while she offers me another cup of tea with some enthusiasm, but I'm wondering what I'm doing here. She hadn't speculated at all on what happened to Michael. I even asked her straight out what she thought, but all she'd said was it was an incredible mystery to her. So I decline the tea, say that I really have to be going. She seems disappointed, but follows me to the entranceway.

As I open the door, I notice that a wet, late November snow is falling. Putting on my coat, Mrs. Huber says, "you better get yourself some galoshes before winter sets in. You'll ruin those shoes."

I don't like galoshes, really. I don't know why, I've just always sort of dogged slushy snow and even walked through it.

"Hmm," I said, not really wanting to have a discussion about galoshes.

Mrs. Huber looks unconvinced.

"Honestly, those are nice enough shoes. They use a lot of salt around here and the salt will leave stains."

She's talking to me as if I've just moved here from Florida. I know about salt stains. I clean them off a few times every winter. And I don't like hassling with rubber galoshes every day.

"Well, you've probably got a point there," I say.

"You can get galoshes at Wackermans Department Store. Wackermans has a storewide 30% off sale going on. Do you know where Wackermans is?"

I don't know where Wackermans is but I do know that I want to get going.

"Yea, I'm pretty sure I know where it is…"

But that's not good enough for her.

"It's easy. Just take a left out of our driveway. At the first traffic light you…"

She's quite animated now, very lively over being able to direct me to Wackermans. I stare dumbly as her words wash over me, and I'm surprised at feeling angry. She's just trying to help, I suppose, but I really hate standing here politely listening to her tell me something that I don't want to know about.

The Missing Persons Department's receptionist is a young and attractive blond, which I imagine might work in my favor. A more experienced receptionist might be a problem. Luckily, there's no one else within earshot.

"Hello, I'm Ed Walker." I'm hopeful that the lettering on my FBI name tag which reads *Finance Department* is too small to be noticed, but she doesn't even seem to look at my tag.

"Hello," she says.

"Just following up on the Michael Huber case. I understand a bum came in here and said he knew where Huber was, but that he left before he gave any information. Sounds like he was a real difficult customer."

Her eyes light up in recognition. "Oh yea, that was so weird."

"Can you tell me what happened? And a description of the bum might be useful."

"I told that other officer," she said.

"Yea, that was agent Teamerson. But like I said, we're just following up on things." My heart is thumping, and I'm beginning to think this was a mistake.

"Well, he was kinda crazy," she says. "He said he knew where that missing guy was but he wanted the reward money right away, and I just told him that he wouldn't get the reward money until it lead to the guy being found, but he was really, like, paranoid about it, and then he got mad and just walked out. Agent Teamerson said the guy probably didn't know anything anyways."

"Yea, Teamerson's probably right about that," I say. What did he look like?"

"Very odd looking. Like one of those Rastafarian guys. Big long dreadlocks and a beard. Not too old. Maybe in his twenties. Really skinny and tattoos all over his arms."

I can't help smiling and I think *Teamerson, you are one lazy ass.* Every day I take the same bus to work and my stop is right across from this park, and there are usually a few homeless types on the benches, talking, some of them drinking wine or high-strength beer. I see that Rastafarian bum hanging out there most days. He's even asked me for change a few times. You can't help noticing someone who looks that strange.

Cathy is in the family room with her friends and they're shrieking with laughter and drinking daiquiris, getting boozed-up for a night out dancing at some club. She'll be sleeping in late tomorrow morning so I need to tell her now that I'm gonna be gone for a few days. I don't know how she'll react – I never do.

I'm wondering what to tell Cathy, but I also find myself thinking about meeting that Rastafarian bum earlier this morning. I just showed him the photo of Michael Huber and a hundred dollars cash.

"You some kinda cop?" he asked.

"Do you want the money?" I said. "I'll give you the hundred, but I need you to tell me where Michael Huber is."

He gave me this pissed-off look, but he didn't take his eye off the cash in my hand either.

"I seen him up at Watertown," the bum said. "I was staying in this park across from the Barnes & Noble bookstore for a couple of weeks, and I seen that guy go in the bookstore. I know it was him. I seen him go in there a lot." I know the bookstore. It's about 45 minutes drive south of here – I've been there a few times myself.

I walk into the family room and stand around, waiting for Cathy and her friends to notice me. One of them is telling some story about peeing in her underpants and she's making a joke about her pelvic floor. I don't know what a pelvic floor is, but apparently it's hilarious because the others are shrieking with laughter and spilling their drinks. I look at Cathy and she's wearing this blue dress made from some sheer material, but I know that she's wearing this stretchy thing underneath which is supposed to hold in the softness around her waist. You're not supposed to notice it, and I'll bet that when Cathy's out on a dark dance floor later tonight you won't spot it, but I've seen it in the laundry. Most of her friends are divorced, which is probably relevant in some manner or other.

"Ed, what is it? Don't just stand there staring," Cathy says, irritation written on her face.

"I just need to let you know I'm out of town for the weekend – I've got a conference I have to go to."

"Whatever, fine, it doesn't matter," she says, turning her back on me.

One of her friends is launching into another story, so I have to raise my voice. "The thing is Cathy, it's out of town, so I'm gonna need to use the car."

"Well, how am I supposed to get around," Cathy says. Yeah, I think, how are you gonna get to your bridge club and drama club and whatever else?

"Maybe a friend could drive," I suggest.

She purses her lips and turns her back on me and they are off to the races again, one of her friends starting a new story, which I'm sure is hilarious.

I'd found a corner table in the Barnes & Noble bookstore café which allowed me to see the store entrance, and I figured Michael would probably read books in the café, so it seemed like the perfect place. All Saturday I nibbled cookies, drank coffee, and peered over a stack of books I was paging through, but there was no Michael. At 7:30 PM I was beginning to think that the Rasta bum was full of crap, but I was also wondering about calling in sick tomorrow, and that's when I saw him walk through the front door. As real as it was, I almost didn't believe it. But it was Michael, same jeans and checked shirt from his photo, except the shirt was a blue-and-white pattern.

Michael disappeared into the store and I had an impulse to follow him, but I stayed put, feeling sure he'd end up in the café.

It's odd, but I felt like I knew his mannerisms already. Fifteen minutes later Michael puts some books on a table not more than 10 feet from me, gets himself a coffee at the counter, and sits down to read. I glance at him now and again over the top of my book for the next few hours, struck by how normal he appears, and how strange that seems – just another guy reading in a bookstore café. I know I've got a decision to make, I just can't be sure exactly when I'll have to make it.

At 10:30 PM I follow Michael out into the parking lot, a cold November rain falling on our faces from a dark sky. He gets into an old Ford and I quick-step my way to my car, feeling very unprepared. My only training in following someone in a car comes from watching TV, but I manage to keep behind Michael for about 4 miles. The traffic makes it a bit challenging and I have to run a red light, but after a while we end up on a dark rural road lined by a wooded area on both sides. This is more worrying because there's no traffic to hide in now, and I don't know how long I can stay behind Michael before he notices me. Maybe he watches out for cars tailing him anyway. And then, suddenly, those twin red tail lights break and his car turns into the woods, probably down a dirt track, and then he stops. I drive on past and pull over a couple of hundred yards farther on.

By the time I get out of my car and peer into the woods, Michael's car lights are off, and he has disappeared into the darkness. I walk carefully back down the road, peering into the bleak forest through rain falling wet on my face, scanning for any sign of Michael. And then, lights appear through the trees. A few minutes later, I find the dirt track and follow it toward the lights, which I am now sure come from two windows. A moment later I am standing next to Michael's Ford and looking at an old trailer home. It's covered in rust and moss and looks like it's been back in these woods for decades. The forest is wet and quiet, and I creep slowly forward. A moment later I can make out Michael's profile through one of the windows, and I realize he's sitting at a table.

The door knob is cold and wet under my fingers, but it turns easily and the door opens quietly. When I step into the entranceway, Michael looks up at me, eyes wide with fear. He's been reading at his table, a cup of coffee in front of him. We stare at one another, neither of us seeming to know what to say. Maybe he never planned for this, and I don't think I've really thought this far ahead.

Finally, he says, "what do you want?"

I don't know how to answer that, really. His eyes look me over, maybe trying to see if I have some weapon on me. Then he scans the room, probably wondering if he can get to some weapon himself.

"Have you come to take me back?" he asks.

"No," I say.

I look down at the linoleum floor, feeling heat and shame crawling up the back of my neck, feeling unhappy that I'm scaring this guy. I look up at Michael, knowing that I have to say something.

"I think I need to tell you about my life," I say. "If that's alright?"

The fear seems to slip a little from his eyes and is replaced with a quizzical expression. He gets up slowly from the table and walks to a counter-top where he gets the coffee pot off the warmer and pours a cup, not taking his eyes off me. He brings the cup back to the table and sets it down, and then re-fills his own cup. He puts the coffee pot back on the warmer and sits at the table, still watching me warily. I'm suddenly aware that the rain is coming down hard on the roof above us, but there are waves of warm air coming off the trailer's heating system which I can feel against my wet face.

"Have a seat, if you want to," he says.

Pretty Bitter

Karen left the note on the kitchen table, a strawberry fridge magnet on top of it.

Dear Dave, you are such a nice guy and you deserve better. I'm gone, I'm afraid. Do you remember Vincenzo, the Pilates teacher at my gym? I think you met him at that barbecue last summer. Anyway, I need to follow my dreams and I think you should too. Can you please look after Mittens for me? There are cans of cat food in the cupboard next to the fridge.

Adieu. Karen XXO

I hold the note limply between my fingers and gaze past it, out through the kitchen window. I should probably think about how Karen is gone, or wonder about how flexible Vincenzo is and what he's been doing with all that bendiness, or maybe I should worry about what Karen is doing with her credit card. But for quite a while, I don't know how long, I'm just numb, my vision glazed and stuck in the middle distance. And, I don't know why, but I'm thinking about Mao Tse-Tung and how he died at the ripe age of 82. In one way or another he killed about 70 million people and then died peacefully in his sleep. It makes me a little mad to think about that.

A lot of people would probably take a few days off work, but I'd just end up sitting around, staring into space. So I went into the lab, and everything around me is just the same as ever.

Experimental epidemiology is pretty low down on the list of what most doctors see as a glamorous career, but I'd fallen into such a specialist area that there's probably nothing else I can do. I spend most of my time doing field work, collecting and analyzing samples related to work staff who may have been exposed to a disease or some contaminant. A lot of jobs are more dangerous than you'd expect. Immigration and customs inspectors (not good), wastewater treatment plant operators (not good), podiatrists (it's diseased feet, for Christ's sake), dental hygienists (stay away). And flight attendants? Routinely spending hours in a confined and concealed environment with a couple of hundred people who have been traveling to far away places (really not good).

Two solid waste collectors (okay, garbage men) lifted a mystery bag over their heads, which had broken and dumped something very smelly all over them – so I'm analyzing this nasty gunk when my phone rings. Our receptionist tells me it's someone calling from a film company.

"Hello, this is Dr. Martin Shaw," I say.

"Hiya Dr. Shaw. My name is Bernie Andrews. I'm a film director and I work for Extreme Studios. We're an adult entertainment company. Anyway, I'm making a new film series which is a bit unusual, and the people in the legal department think I should get someone in to give us an opinion, you know, about health and safety. I hear you're just the man."

"Adult entertainment...?" I ask.

"Yeah, you know, porn."

"Oh," I say, and think, *well, this is a first.* "Are you concerned about disease transmission among your... what do you call them? Actors?"

"Sure, actors... actresses. Disease transmission sounds a little extreme, but yeah, Legal wants us to get this checked out."

76

Sounds a little extreme. I consider pointing out that his film company is called *Extreme* Studios, but I'm too tired to care and it's doubtful he'd appreciate the irony. We make an appointment for 2 days time.

I see the dead bird as I pull into my driveway. It's splayed out right in the middle of the asphalt and I stop the car in front of it. I get out and inspect it closely. It's a finch, dead eyes glazed and staring past me into who knows what. Sharp claws have ripped and bloodied its chest and there are tiny downy feathers lying around it. If it weren't so dead I imagine it would be thinking, *I did not see that coming.* I should probably do something about it.

I get myself a few cold beers from the fridge, a glass, some crackers and cheese, and take everything out onto the front porch. I settle into an Adirondack deck chair and pour one of the beers. If you're in a bad frame of mind and you have a couple of extra beers it saves you the trouble of getting up to get another one. That's a time-saving tip. There is a lot of birdsong in the air but it's frenetic and urgent, and somehow I think they are not too concerned about the fellow lying out there in the driveway. People think birdsong is beautiful – some people even write poems about it. Birdsong is never about anything except sex and territory, but that's not what the poems are about.

I wasn't gonna call Karen, but after I finished most of the second beer it started to seem like a good idea. She is following her dreams because she has to, but maybe those dreams weren't making her so happy after all. You never know. I pull my cell phone from a pocket. It rings for a while and then I get her normal message, her tone bubbly and flirty.

Hiya lovelies. Karenkins here. When you hear the beep don't be a creep – leave me a message! Love yaaaaaa!
Beeeeep.

I hang up and notice Mittens the cat walking slowly along the porch railing in that unconscious and perfectly balanced way which should impress me, but I'm thinking about what happened to that Finch. Mittens stares at me impassively. *Kitty's Salmon Chunks* at $2.25 a can is for dinner – tearing a finch to pieces is just for fun, isn't it Mittens? For fun and for show.

I'm almost done with my third beer when something occurs to me. Karen's phone rang for a while before it went to the answering service, which makes me think she ignored my call. I take a swig of beer. The Finch is still dead out in the driveway and the birdsong seems even louder. I should probably get the shovel out of the garage and do something about that bird. I should probably try and figure out how to get Karen back too, but for some reason I find myself thinking about the Roman-Jewish wars, maybe because birds were involved. In what is now Palestine the Jews and Greeks kept up a pretty constant exchange of insults, and then one day around 66 AD there was a full-scale riot and a lot of stuff got smashed up. The Roman governor tried to make the Jews pay for the damage, but the Jews claimed the Greeks were to blame for sacrificing some Pigeons on the steps of *their* synagogue. The Jews refuse to pay, the Romans insist, the Jews revolt, and 350,000 die. Message: Don't screw with the Romans.

The birds are really making a racket now and I realize I need to take a piss. Maybe I should just take a piss in the middle of my front yard. It's my god-damned yard, isn't it?

But I know I won't.

Most of the 350,000 that died were just citizens caught up in events – that's how it is. It makes me a little mad to think about that.

The waiting room at Extreme Studios is not what I was expecting. Maybe I imagined that the world of pornography would be seedy, but the couch is leather, the fittings shiny, the woodwork genuine, and the receptionist pleasant and professional. I might as well be waiting to see a lawyer or family doctor. The only giveaway is the porn industry awards on the wall and shelves.

A young woman, maybe 18 or 19, walks in. Long blond hair, shimmering blue eyes, thin. You sort of wonder if women that beautiful actually exist, so it's surprising when one walks right past you. She greets the receptionist in a way which tells me she's an insider and then disappears through a door into the heart of the building.

The receptionist's voice pulls me out of my trance. "Dr. Shaw, Mr. Andrews is able to see you now."

I pick up my medical bag and follow her down a hallway to a door with a plaque which reads, *Bernie Andrews DIRECTOR*. She opens the door, introduces me, smiles, and disappears back down the hallway.

He's up out of his chair, leaning over his desk with an outstretched hand. "Dr. Shaw, very good of you to come. Bernie Andrews."

We shake hands and I notice that the office has all the good taste and effects of the reception area. Bernie is casually dressed, short and chubby with a well-trimmed beard and a big smile.

"Hello," I say. We sit down. "So, what sort of help are you looking for?"

Bernie leans back in his chair, appearing very relaxed. He smiles again and directs an index finger at me. "Straight to the point – I like that."

On the wall behind Bernie, I notice what must be about a hundred framed promotional shots of women, mainly naked from the waist up, most likely the porn stars he's worked with. It strikes me as pretentious, but then I recall that most doctors like to cover their consulting room wall in diplomas.

"So here's the thing Dr. Shaw – I'm gonna be shooting a new series called *Teen Ass to BJ*. It's not a completely new idea in the industry, but it's probably the first time anyone has shot a whole series along these lines, so our legal people are telling me we need to get some advice. You know, just to make sure our disclaimer forms are up to date."

This is a lot to take in. "Uhm, Mr. Andrews... ."

"Oh please," he says, that big grin still on his face. "Call me Bernie. You call me Mr. Andrews and I feel like you're sitting in the next room."

"Uhm, okay Bernie. Look – I don't really know a lot about pornography. What is... teen ass to BJ?"

"Yeah, well it mainly follows the form of most anal porn scenes, so it's a 25 to 35 minute shoot, the girl herself, undressing, blow job, sex, and the money shot – but with one twist. During the scene we're alternating anal with blow jobs. Ya see, the guy is getting a blow job, then he's doing anal, and then he goes straight back into a blow job, then more anal, and so on. That's what makes the series different. It's kind of a niche we wanna explore more."

I catch my reflection in one of the framed photos behind Bernie and I notice that my mouth is hanging open and my eyebrows are pulled together – I look either idiotic or stunned, or maybe both. I close my mouth and try to express something like intelligence.

"Okay," I say. "So you want information about potential negative health effects of this... sort of film?"

"If that's how you want to put it."

I look down at Bernie's desk, considering the risks of what he's describing to me. "So... will the male actor be using a condom?"

"I guess you don't know much about porn, do you?" he says, a friendly grin on his face.

"Okay," I say. "So when the guy... uhm... you know, is alternating from the one thing to the other, are you going to have some way of sanitizing his... penis?"

"I'd like to doc, but I can't do it. Breaks up the scene. If you've got a camera break during the scene, however cleanly you try to do it, it's obvious what happened. Porn viewers are pretty sophisticated these days."

A sophisticated porn viewer? I think. What in the world is that?

"Bernie," I say, "there are reasonably effective methods of sterilization which can mitigate against disease... are you sure..."

Bernie is shaking his head. "Give the people what they want – that's my motto. I can't stop the scene for sterilizing or sanitizing or if the building catches fire."

We gaze at each other for a moment and I'm aware again of this ache I get, right in the middle of my chest. I used to think it was indigestion. I guess it's worse since Karen left, but if I'm honest it's been there for a while. If I didn't have a medical degree, I'd probably go see my doctor. But I know just what tests they'd do and that they'd tell me there's nothing wrong with my heart, at least not medically.

Bernie spreads his arms wide and smiles again. "So what do you think, Doc?"

"Well, the way I work is I take samples on site and then I analyze them at the lab, and then you get a report."

"Oh," says Bernie, looking a bit surprised. "Can't you just give us an opinion, you know, something which the legal folks can use?"

"I guess you don't know much about epidemiology," I say, and I try to replicate Bernie's smile.

Bernie laughs. "Okay, so you don't want to just give us an opinion?"

81

"An opinion based on what?" I say. "I don't imagine there's much medical research which has examined what you're proposing."

Bernie smiles. "And you wanna take samples? Well, this is gonna be interesting." He checks his watch. "Okay Doc, let's do it."

"What, now?" I say.

He sticks his index finger at me again and grins. "The porn industry moves fast. If I don't make this series now, some other shit stain will do it within a couple of months."

He springs from his chair and leads me down the hallway. I'm not sure I want to follow, but there is something about Bernie's energy which carries me along and I imagine he affects others in the same way. We walk through two sets of doors and onto what is clearly a movie set. I notice bright stage lights with those dark umbrellas behind them, two cameras on tripods, a thick throw rug on the floor, and what appears to be a sparsely decorated living room with a black leather couch in the middle. Three guys are sitting in chairs off to the side, chatting to each other and drinking coffee. One of the men is in his briefs, handsome, muscled, and tanned.

"Okay guys," says Bernie. "Change of plans. Where's Vicca?"

"She's still in make-up," one of the guys says.

Bernie walks to a wall and pulls back a curtain. "Vicca sweetheart, you almost ready?"

"Yes, yes," a voice responds, feminine and with a thick accent which sounds Eastern European.

Bernie turns to face us, smiling. "I spend all my life waiting for a woman, and it's worth every minute, isn't that right Vicca?"

"Yes, yes, I am now coming."

A moment later she enters. The young woman who walked past me in reception is standing in front of us. Her blond hair has been done into long pigtails and she is wearing a pink skirt which is so short it reveals white silk panties. On top she's got on a semi-transparent negligee. She totters over to us on impossible high heels. I'm suddenly aware that I'm gripping the handle of my medical bag quite hard.

Bernie turns to address us and I notice that the men and Vicca all give their attention to him. This seems wrong. When a woman like that, dressed like that, walks into a room, I would think the world would stop, people would stare, people would applaud. But they all act as if they have seen it a hundred times, and maybe they have.

"Okay people," says Bernie. "This is Dr. Shaw – he's gonna be taking some samples during our shoot today. It's for health and safety, so just let him do what he needs to. But we got a change of plans. We're not shooting Teen Anal 36. We're gonna do a trial shoot of Teen Ass to BJ."

Bernie looks over at the guy in his briefs. "Mike, you're scheduled for a Teen Ass to BJ scene next week – you know the sequence, right?" Mike nods.

He looks over at Vicca. "Vicca sweetheart just follow Mike's lead, okay. You've done blow jobs with gagging before, haven't you?" Vicca looks a bit confused. "I don't be sure," she says.

"Vicca, you know gagging," says Mike. "Remember when we did Teen Sluts?" Vicca still looks confused.

"Gagging... like this," says Mike. Mike opens his mouth and thrusts his fist back and forth in front of his mouth a few times and then makes a gagging sound he produces from the back of his throat.

Vicca nods in recognition. "Oh yes, I know."

I'm sitting in my deck chair, beer in hand, crackers and cheese on the table. This evening I got two extra beers out, and they're next to me, beads of condensation running down the cans. The birds are as noisy as ever, soliciting and threatening, and I notice that the dead finch in the driveway is gone. Some other animal must have taken him, and there isn't the smallest sign that he was ever there, or ever existed.

Bernie's film happened just as he described it, but with a brutality I did not anticipate. The images play themselves out in front of me. Gagging blow jobs? That was Vicca choking for air. *What seems bizarre to most people – well, in the porn world maybe that's just what happens.* And there I was, right in it, stepping over camera wires, using cotton swabs on Mike's enormous penis, Vicca's mouth, vagina, and anus, doing my job the way it needs to be done. What people don't get when they watch this stuff at home is the odor. The sweat, the body fluids, and I think for Vicca, the fear and pain. I want to imagine Vicca the way I first saw her in reception, but that's difficult now.

I must have been lost in my thoughts for a while because my third beer is almost gone, and I have this heavy sense of not knowing what to do this evening, or maybe tomorrow evening. I pull my cell phone from my pocket and dial, trying not to think about the decision I'm making. It rings for a while.

Hiya lovelies. Karenkins here. When you hear the beep don't be a creep - leave me a message! Love yaaaaaa!
Beeeeep.

I hang up, go into the kitchen, open the fridge, and gaze at the 2 cold beers I've got left. I close the door and slowly make my way up to my bedroom. I get down on one knee, pull a floorboard up, and get the box of Hydrocodone. I go back downstairs, pull the beers out of the fridge and put them on the porch table, and then consider what to do with the box of pills. I want to be able to look at them, so I place the box carefully on the porch railing, right in front of me. I pour a beer slowly into my glass and for some perverse reason, this all seems like the right thing to do, maybe the only thing to do.

It's true what they say about doctors having a higher rate of suicide than the general public. Maybe it's stress they say, maybe it's a personality type they say – but I don't think so. Doctors just have access to very easy and painless ways to die. I bet we don't want to die more than other people, it's just that dying is so darn difficult when you're not a doctor. It was about 18 months ago when I noticed an invoice for 5 boxes of Hydrocodone at work, and wouldn't you know it, there were six. When is a missing box not a missing box? That's a morbid riddle.

I don't know why, but for a moment I see myself from the outside – see myself from the point of view of someone standing in the middle of my yard and watching this guy sitting on the porch, this guy guzzling beer and staring at a box with enough pills to put down a horse. What seems bizarre to most people – well, in my world maybe that's just what happens.

I remember something which occurred right near they end of the porn scene. Vicca had really taken a pounding. The context was different than an assault and robbery in a back alley, but the quality of the experience must have been similar. But you didn't see the real experience, not *her* real experience. Throughout the scene, she had been able to create a pretense that she was fine, that she even liked what was happening to her. But there was this moment when the pain and humiliation broke through. Her eyes had watered with the effort and black smudges of make-up had run down her cheeks, and for maybe 3 seconds it had got to be too much and I saw her humanness and the pain in her expression – eyebrows pulled together in distress and frustration, the corners of her mouth twisting into a macabre grimace. The moment passed quickly and she pulled herself together and got back on script. *I don't know, maybe you reach a point where you can't do it anymore.*

I take a gulp of beer and gaze at the box of pills. There is some text which reads *may cause drowsiness. Do not operate heavy machinery while using.* I guess I can comply with that. Maybe I'll just keep drinking for a while and see what happens. The bank statement came today. I should probably open it but I'm pretty sure it will read like a holiday itinerary, like a diary Karen is keeping about the booze and hotels and distractions. I should probably do something about it. I don't know why but I find myself thinking about the 100 Years War. A hundred years of the French and the English killing each other, and it wasn't about anything except royal families trying to come out on top. Charles the Mad is a good example. He was riding one day with his entourage and something startled him so he just started swinging his sword at everyone in his party – killed four attendants who didn't even think to defend themselves. He went to a masked ball once dressed as a wild shaggy man and accidently set fire to himself and a few others, and some woman sat on top of him and smothered the flames with her dress. That probably wasn't comfortable for her. But it's not funny when 3.5 million people die because of all this nonsense. They even burned Joan of Arc on that pyre. It makes me a little mad to think about that.

I hand my report to Bernie. I thought he might at least give it a cursory read, but he just puts it on his desk.

"It's nice of you to drop off the report Doc, but you could have just mailed it."

"I wanted to give you a verbal report as well," I say. Bernie makes a show of looking at his watch.

"Pretty busy schedule today. Is it fairly quick?"

I frown. "Bernie, what I saw the other day will of course expose both actors to the normal range of STDs. Chlamydia, genital herpes, HIV, gonorrhea, as well as hepatitis A."

Bernie shakes his head and waves his hands. "All covered Doc. Our actors and actresses get tested regularly for that stuff. It's an industry standard."

"That's good," I say. "And the samples I took from both Vicca and Mike didn't reveal any of those diseases. But this new niche you're wanting to explore, this ass to BJ stuff, raises something else. Escherichia coli... E. coli. It's a bacteria which lives in the human digestive system, but it's supposed to stay there, and the films you want to make will likely mean that it's going to end up in places it's not supposed to."

"Okay," says Bernie. "It's in the report, right?"

"Yeah, but what I'm saying is that if E. coli gets transferred from the lower digestive tract to elsewhere, you can get urinary tract infections. There's a certain strain of E. coli which can give you severe diarrhea. There's another strain which is not very common called 0157:H7, and that one could give you anemia or even kidney disease."

"Yea, well you should have been around during AIDS. Now that was a bitch of a time for the industry."

"Bernie, I found traces of E. coli in Vicca's vagina and mouth."

"Oh," he says. "Was it the bad kind of E. coli or was it cool?"

I want to say something which would wipe the smile off Bernie's face, which would make him consider what he's doing, but more important than that is my need to be a good scientist. Whatever my inadequacies as a human being, that is something I've always had, and being a good scientist means being honest.

"Bernie, there aren't really any *cool* strains of E. coli, but no, what I found was a strain of E. coli which isn't especially worrying. Vicca's immune and excretory systems will probably manage it. But other strains could be worse."

"And that's why I'm gonna send your report to the legal people, and they can use it to update the disclaimer forms our actors and actresses sign, and everyone's happy."

"Bernie, you think people like Vicca will want to sign a disclaimer form with that sort of information?"

Bernie looks a bit weary. "Probably, but to be honest Doc I don't know. I just shoot films and sometimes I do what the legal department tells me to…"

Someone pounds on his office door and suddenly there's this bare-footed woman in a pink bathrobe standing next to me, glaring and shouting at Bernie. "Trinity took my fucking lube again Bernie. It was on the table in make-up and I know she was shooting yesterday!"

"Cindy, we got boxes and boxes of lube around this place," says Bernie.

This woman juts a hip at Bernie and blood runs into her face. "Bernie," she yells, "you know I bring my own lube and it's scented, and Trinity took it. You have to tell that slut to STOP DOING IT."

Bernie grins and raises his hands. "Who cares if the lube is scented?" He looks over at me. "Do you care if your lube is scented?"

"Just tell her not to touch my fucking lube Bernie," she shouts. The woman turns on a bare heel and slams the door.

Bernie sighs deeply. "Doc, I really got a lot to do."

The taxi driver doesn't seem too happy that I'm drinking beer in the back of his car, but he's not saying anything about it. I wonder if this is my third or fourth beer. I check my watch as he pulls over – 7:45 PM.

"Number 208 is somewhere across the street," the driver says, pointing at a row of older houses. I pay him and get out. There's a bench on my side of the street, so I sit down and scan the houses opposite, houses bathed in fading evening light. Vicca's neighborhood is like so many you find in the inner city – run down, litter on the sidewalks, disused junk in the front yards, a cinderblock bar on the corner with a flashing neon light. I scan Vicca's paperwork again to make sure I've got the address right. After the porn scene, I spoke briefly with Mike and Vicca about their medical histories, and a doctor always takes contact information.

I take a large swig of my beer and find I'm playing three images through my mind. The Vicca I saw in reception – beautiful, vibrant, innocent. The Vicca I saw throughout most of the porn scene – a woman participating in a terrible game of pretend. The Vicca I saw for about 3 seconds when the game of pretend broke down – beautiful, innocent, and victimized. I shouldn't be here, but for some reason I need confirmation that there is still some decency, some goodness left in this world.

I trip on the front step and realize I'm a bit more drunk than I thought. A heavy throb of bass music comes from the other side of the door, so I knock loudly to be sure I can be heard. The door opens a few inches but catches on a chain. Vicca stares at me through the gap.

"Who are you?" she asks. Above the throb of the bass music, I can hear a dog growling and snapping behind the door.

"It's Dr. Shaw, from Extreme Studios. I took some samples."

I notice a glimmer of recognition. Vicca shuts the door, pulls the chain back, and opens the door about halfway. The dog looks like some hideous mix of Doberman and Rottweiler, and continues to growl at me.

Her hair is disheveled, her sweatshirt dirty, and her face looks pasty without the make-up. But she is still beautiful, if you know how to look for it. A siren erupts and then fades down a nearby street.

"What do you want?" she asks.

"I was just in the neighborhood and I thought… ."

A deep male voice shouts something from inside. "Kas fuck ir tas, ka?"

Vicca turns her head and shouts back, "Ta sir neviens!"

When she turns to face me again, I notice her eyes. Once in a while I do work for one of the needle exchange programs in the city, usually because there's been a needle-stick injury or some contamination worry. Vicca's eyes are drooping and her facial muscles are flaccid. It's unmistakable – the look of opiate use, heroin.

"I'm sorry to bother you," I say.

A male figure appears behind Vicca. A big guy, but overweight and wearing a beard, maybe 10 years older than Vicca. "To, ko fuck vins grib?" he says to Vicca.

"Vins nevienam, neuztraucieties," Vicca says to him. He scows at me and trudges back down the hallway.

I take a step backward. "I'm very sorry. It's much too late to be visiting. I'll leave you alone." She looks a little perplexed and annoyed. The door slams closed, the chain lock slides across, and I hear the dog going mad as if he is attacking the other side of the door.

I'm sitting in my deck chair, gazing out at the lawn, drinking and thinking. I've drunk three beers and I've got cheese and crackers and two more cold ones on the table next to me. I can barely remember what happened at work today. Oh, I got the lab results back on those two garbage men who lifted the mystery bag that spilled all over them. It was horseshit – a big bag of decomposing and runny horseshit. I take a gulp of beer. Isn't that just life?

I don't think Vicca was any of those images I had of her. Victim, perpetrator, innocent, guilty, pretend, real? Maybe she is all and none of those things. Maybe I have no idea of what I'm talking about. I take another gulp of beer and a bite of cracker and cheese. She was beautiful, though. That's something I can say which is true.

I get up out of my chair and walk to the bedroom. I pull the floorboard up and take the box of Hydrocodone downstairs and over to the kitchen counter. It's funny how you can do something and yet it's almost like you didn't even decide to do it. It's like you're just all behavior without anything behind it. Maybe these moments happen because you actually made the decision a long time ago. I pour about 12 ounces of orange juice into a blender and then I add a couple of spoonfuls of sugar because the pills are going to be pretty bitter. Pretty bitter, pretty bitter, pretty bitter. It's like a little mantra you can sing to yourself forever. Isn't that nice?

I pop 60 of the Hydrocodone out of their blister packs and drop them one at a time into the juice. Thirty might not do the job – 90 might make me vomit before full ingestion. Science, you see? I wonder why they call them blister packs? Medicine is supposed to get rid of pain, but blisters hurt. Let's add this contradiction to the list of stupid shit that doesn't make sense. I get the blender going and stare out the kitchen window. Karen's note is still on the table. I didn't want to keep it but I didn't want to throw it out either. Does that make sense?

I take the pint of juice onto the porch, place it on the side table, and sit in my deck chair. Bars and clubs like to have fun names for the drinks they serve. I'll call mine *A Sleep Forever*. Excuse me, can I have a sleep forever, please? I guess it's not a very fun name.

I take my cell phone out of my pocket and stare at it for a few moments. This is a big one. As it's ringing my heart starts pounding, really banging against the inside of my ribs. I'd like to have more control over my physiology, being a doctor and all. Five rings…. six rings…

Hiya lovelies. Karenkins here. When you hear the beep don't be a creep – leave me a message! Love yaaaaaa!

Beeeeep.

I hang up. The evening light is fading. It's that strange time right between day and night, twilight, I guess. Or dusk. But there is something odd about *this* evening. I gaze into the still air, and then it hits me. The birds are quiet. I look around and notice that they are up in the trees, but they're just sitting on the branches. I'd like to think that maybe they are quiet out of respect, out of respect for my situation. But I'm too good a scientist for that. There must be something about the weather or something which is happening in their bird community to explain it. I know it's not about me. I take a sip of Sleep Forever. It's still too bitter – I should have added more sugar. But perfecting a suicide drink is a little difficult, for obvious reasons.

My report to Extreme Studios won't change anything because no one wants anything to change. Mittens kills because she feels like it. Vicca shoots heroin because she needs it. Somebody is going to take somebody's lube. E. coli does whatever is necessary to survive and reproduce. And Karen isn't coming back because she doesn't want to. The world changes and everything remains the same.

I take another sip of Sleep Forever. Ya know, in the early 1800's France had a standing quarrel with Algeria over the slave trade and some debt. They might have sorted it out, but one day Hussein, the ruler of Algeria, gets annoyed with the French consul and smacks him across the face with his fly whisk. It was probably pretty hot, being Algeria. And so, France invades Algeria and 775,000 die, mostly people who didn't want anything to do with it. It makes me a little made to think about that.

Going Back to the Beginning

Twenty-two years of practicing psychotherapy and I've had some low moments, moments where I wasn't sure I saw the point anymore, but right now is probably about as pissed-off as I've ever felt. I check my watch as I leave the office – 10:45 AM. I've got 15 minutes before my next patient arrives. I don't really have enough time to get a newspaper, but I need to get the hell away from this place.

The city street is full of pedestrians, all of them seeming to walk with a sense of urgency, a sense of purpose. Good for them. There are so many people on the sidewalk I have to pick a course through this mass of limbs and movement. I don't want to think about my first two patients I saw this morning, but the images and feelings got inside my head. You're professional, you see, so there are certain things you feel and think during a session, but you don't say them because it's your job to be sensitive *and* empathetic *and* patient *and*... a lot of things.

My 9:00 AM appointment was a guy I'd seen for about 15 sessions. Medicaid was paying for his therapy, which was going exactly nowhere. He is what I think of as a *burnt-out antisocial personality disorder*. Fifty-two years old and he no longer has the physical health to brutalize society with his behavior or his own body with drugs and booze. A lifetime of school expulsion and behavioral units, petty theft, assault, producing children he can't support, and a shed-load drugs and alcohol. But he still has enough vitality to hurl his paranoid rants at me about how everyone and everything has screwed *him* over. Any attempt I make to help him see that he is in some small way responsible for

93

his problems is met with a fresh wave of accusations. And, I'm quite sure he thinks his psychotherapist is an idiot. I don't know how to help this guy. Patients are good at getting you to feel as they feel. That's analytic theory for dummies. But I'm sick of feeling angry – angry at him for being such a useless patient and angry at myself for being such a useless therapist. Not caring sometimes seems like a viable alternative. Perhaps apathy *is* the last great defense.

I arrive at the shop, collect my newspaper, and go through the mechanics of making the purchase. Back out on the street, I check my watch – 10:51 AM. Nine minutes before my next appointment. It's a new patient and I haven't even read the referral letter. I'll be late to the appointment, which, despite my mood, matters to me. I quicken my pace and weave a path through this morning's salmon run of pedestrians. I think about the 10:00 AM patient I'd just seen. A 32-year-old woman from a wealthy family with anorexia. We are 27 sessions into our work and I could set my watch by the trajectory this therapy is taking. She is polite, grateful, works hard inside and outside of therapy, does everything I suggest, makes insight… and just keeps losing weight! If she looses 1 more pound, her psychiatrist will pull the plug, pack her off to the eating disorders inpatient unit, and I will have officially failed. Recently, she has told me I was a great therapist and that it's not my fault. I'm very sure she is wrong. I don't know how to help this woman. At the beginning of my career, I was naive and probably a crap therapist. But I felt so sure there was a vital purpose to what I was doing. Sometimes I want to go back to the beginning.

There is an elderly man about 10 feet ahead of me who suddenly goes down. Not agile enough to break his fall, his temple smacks into the pavement and he just lies there. Before I reach him, a half-dozen people walk past, gazing at his crumpled figure. *Bystander effect*, I think. Perfect example. The more people are present in an emergency situation, the less likely any individual will help. Social Psychology 101. But this isn't a classroom, and I'm late for my appointment. Shit. I crouch down over the guy and see that he's conscious, his hazy eyes blinking in the morning light. And then I see this purple-blue swelling coming up on his temple, growing into the size of an egg, blood running down his face. I put my hand on his arm.

"Sir," I say. He nods faintly at me. "You've had a fall. Can you hear me?"

He nods vaguely. His face is deeply wrinkled and I notice that his walking cane is stuck under him in an awkward way. He must be at least 90.

"Can you help me up?" he rasps. Someone bumps against me, trying to get past. A few people have stopped to watch and are chatting to each other and pointing. The purple-blue egg is even larger now and I can see a vein pulsing through it. I look around, wondering if someone might show some interest in giving me a hand. I had a wretched back injury a few years ago, and I need to be careful about lifting or I can be in pain for weeks. I'm not happy about this.

I sense someone next to me and look up. It's a woman, maybe 30 years old. "Do you need some help?" she says.

"Yes please," I say.

She takes one of the old guy's arms, I get the other, and we lift in unison. He's on his feet and the three of us stand there, wondering what to do. "How are you feeling Sir?" I say. The old guy forces a smile, which looks a little macabre with all that blood running down his face. "I'm... I'm..." he starts, and then looks around him. He's groggy and probably concussed. "I need to get home – I'm okay," he says. The woman and I make eye contact and silently acknowledge the same thought. *You are not okay.*

"Sir," the woman says. "You've got quite a bump on your head. I think someone is going to have to look at that."

"I just live over there," the old man says, and he points a tremulous finger down the street. "Belvedere House. I just need to get home and I'll be fine."

I glance at my watch, 10:57 AM, and think about my next appointment. I look up the street and can see what I imagine is the housing unit he's pointing at. It's about 100 yards away. I think about the therapeutic frame. After all the years I've done this job, the therapeutic frame is as much a habit as tying your shoes in the morning. The therapeutic frame is to psychotherapy what the resurrection is to Christianity. The client can act out their pathology in every way they need to, but the therapist must maintain the frame, must keep in place the boundaries and principles which ensure that therapy is not just another social event. Being on time is an essential part of the frame.

"I'm just going to get his cane," the woman says. She keeps hold of his arm as she reaches down and picks up the cane. She looks at her watch and seems a bit apprehensive. "Do you want my help getting him home?" she asks.

I can walk him to his home, but if he goes down again, I'm not sure I can manage. "Do you mind?" I say. "Okay," she replies.

We all walk together and the old guy needs a lot of support because he keeps stepping as if he has no idea where his foot is supposed to hit the pavement. He seems embarrassed that he needs help. "What's your name?" she says to the old man. "What?" he says. "What is your name?" she says, louder this time. "Bobby Ferguson," he says.

She's better at this than I am, I think, and I'm glad she stopped. His weight falls one way and the other and I don't know if it's his age or the head injury, but he's got no balance at all. The woman and I develop a rhythm of taking his weight from one step to the other, and we look at each other now and again to

96

coordinate things between us. As we approach his building, I wonder if it's an assisted living arrangement. I'm hoping it is because we could leave him with staff. I see what must be the entrance. "Sir," I say. "Is there a reception, with staff that might be able to look after you?"

"That's it," he says. "That's where I live." He didn't understand me and I realize that his hearing is pretty bad.

"Sir," the woman says, "shall we take you to reception – see if someone there can help you?"

We make eye contact and keep him headed for the building entrance, but he just stops. "No, not there," he says, nodding at the entrance. "My apartment is down along that path." He starts his odd goose-stepping gait and heads off down the side of the building. "Sir," I say, raising my voice. "Don't you think we should go to reception? Maybe there is someone who can help you."

"Those guys?" he says. "Oh screw 'em. I don't need help. I just need to get home."

"Sir," the woman says, her tone kind and patient. "If you could see your head, you'd know that someone needs to look at it. I think we are going to need to call the paramedics." The old man nods but I'm pretty sure he didn't hear.

We carry on down the path and a moment later he points to a door. "That's my place," he says. I try the door handle, but it's locked. "Have you got a key sir," the woman says.

"My pocket," he says. She hesitates for a moment and then carefully reaches into a front pant pocket and pulls out a handful of Kleenex and a single key.

She manages to get the key into the lock, and with some trial and error we figure out that if I hold one arm and pull the latch handle down while she holds the other arm and turns the key, we can get the door open without dropping the old fellow. Inside, the front living room area is every stereotype of an older person's home. Framed pictures, trinkets and souvenirs of distant memories, and a very old TV set. We place him gently on his couch and look at each other.

"One of us needs to call the paramedics," I say.

"I know," she says.

I look down at Bobby. The wound is still bleeding and I imagine we need to apply some pressure to it. An expression of uncertainty comes across her face, and in a lowered and apologetic tone she says, "I'm late for an appointment."

I nod. "So am I." We stare at each other for a moment, neither sure what to do.

"Look, I'll call," I say. I pull my cell phone from my pocket and dial 911. I imagine she will probably head off. I wouldn't blame her. In a city this size everyone is always late for something. She's helped a lot as it is. She hesitates, but then disappears into a bathroom and I can hear the water running.

"911, what's your emergency please?"

"Hi, my name is Dan Phillips. I was walking down the street and there was an elderly gentleman who fell. He's hit his head pretty hard and there's a large swelling and quite a lot of bleeding…"

The guy asks me a series of questions and I'm answering them the best I can. The woman returns from the bathroom with a warm and damp washcloth. She sits next to the old man on the couch and gently places the washcloth against the wound, holding it there.

"They want to know your address Bobby," I say loudly.

"I'll be just fine," says Bobby. "They been here before but I don't need 'em."

The woman hands me a bill that was on the coffee table. "The address is on this," she says. She's very capable, I think. I look at my watch – 11:06 AM. They keep asking me more questions about Bobby's state and I wish they would just send a paramedic rather than wasting all this time.

The woman is asking Bobby about the photos on the mantle place and coffee table. He's too hard of hearing to understand most of her questions, so she picks a photo up and shows it to him.

"That's Margaret and our boys, Tom and Richard. Margaret had cancer… Tom lives in Seattle now and Richard is in Florida – Miami." He points to Margaret. "Sixty-two years we were together."

"Wow, that's a long time," the woman says. She pulls the washcloth back and has a look at the wound, and then places it back on his head. She points to another photo on the coffee table. There are three young men in the black and white image, all in army uniform. The men are standing on what looks like a beach and I presume one of the men is Bobby, but the men are so young it's hard to tell.

"Were you in the army?" she asks.

"That's Normandy," he says. "Utah Beach." He points to the men in the image. "That's Mike. He died a few years ago. That's Peter, he didn't make it back from France at all. And that's me, in the middle. We were US 4th Infantry."

They keep asking me more questions. Is he conscious? Is he breathing freely? I answer them as quickly as I can, growing irritated. The woman carries on speaking with Bobby in this easy and natural way which I have never found easy *or* natural. I check my watch – 11:12 AM. I really have to go.

"Look," I say to the 911 operator. "I'm really late for an appointment – can you just send a paramedic please?" They agree and tell me they are sending the paramedic now, but insist on asking a couple of more questions.

The woman pulls back the washcloth. "The bleeding has stopped," she says. I notice her glance at her watch.

99

"Excuse me," I say to the operator. I look at the woman. "The paramedic is on the way. They just have a couple more questions. You go if you need to."

The woman seems uncertain for a moment, and then turns and looks at the old man. "Bobby, I have to go now but I'll stop back and check on you later," she says, speaking loudly to ensure she can be understood.

"You can visit anytime," Bobby says.

I'm surprised at the warmth of her gesture. In a city of more than 8 million, that's a rare thing. She walks past me to the door, and we acknowledge each other through smiles and head nods, and then she leaves and is swallowed up in the sea of pedestrians out in the street.

I enter my office at 11:17 AM and catch our receptionist's eye. "Sorry," I say. "It's a long story."

"You're in consulting room 6," she says.

I consider taking another 5 minutes to read the referral letter and decide it's better to just wing it. I get to my desk, open my datebook, and get the patient's name. I quick-step my way to the waiting room and stop. There is one patient sitting in there. A lot of what happens at work is like a ritual. The things you say, when you say them. Like greeting a patient in the waiting room for the first time. *Hello, I'm Dr. Phillips, would you like to come this way?* But I don't know what to say at all as I look at this woman.

"It's you," she says finally, an incredulous expression forming on her face.

"Yes, yes it is," I say.

For a moment there is a space between us where there are no words, and then I fall back on habit. "Diane Knight?" She nods. "I'm Dr. Phillips. Would you like to come this way?"

She follows me to the consulting room. I close the door and we sit down. What happens next is just what you might imagine,

100

which is why it doesn't really matter. We acknowledge the strangeness of our experience, and we express mutual gratitude for each other's help in dealing with Bobby's head injury. We admit the oddness of being late for the same appointment. It takes all of 2 minutes.

And then we slip quietly into roles which are preordained.

I become a therapist – she becomes a patient. Because that's what needs to happen. She tells me about her life and of course her presentation is unique, they all are. But in many ways she is like so many I have seen over so many years. Her problems are complex, long-standing, and serious. Therapy will probably be very difficult.

Following the session I make myself a cup of strong coffee, let the office receptionist know where I'm going, and then step out of the back entrance to the building. The sun is shining and I sit on the step, gaze into space, and drink my coffee. The door opens and a colleague, Janet, steps out. She has a cup in her hand as well.

"Mind if I join you," she says. She looks exasperated, and I'm guessing her morning has not gone so well.

"Sure," I say, and I move over on the step.

"Unbelievable," she says.

"What's that?" I ask.

"My 11 o'clock, Marjory Ashdown, you know her?"

I nod. "Yea, I worked with Marjory about 5 years ago. Hard to forget."

"So Marjory's in another abusive relationship," says Janet. "She's not going to leave this guy of course, so I've been talking about the need for her to be more assertive. So Marjory decides the best way for her to assert herself is to take this guy's toothbrush and use it to clean out the toilet bowl every night. And this guy has no idea what she's doing with his toothbrush. So today I'm trying to explore whether there are other ways, more functional ways, of being assertive, but she really likes the toothbrush approach. She's pretty pleased with herself. Some days I really don't know if I can help these people."

I look at my colleague. "It's frustrating, isn't it?"

She gazes back at me. "Yea, it really is." She is still looking at me and a puzzled expression forms on her face.

"What's up with you?" she says. "You seem different."

I take a sip of coffee, close my eyes, and look up into the warmth of the sun. "I feel different," I say.

I look back at my colleague. She's still wearing a puzzled expression.

"This job, it's maddening," I say. "But... something happened to me this morning, something strange. Do you wanna hear about it?"

Note to reader: There is a line which reads *Perhaps apathy is the last great defense*. This idea is attributed to the American psychologist Rollo May.

The Treatment

I am wrenched into wakefulness and sit up in bed. Gazing down through the half-light at Howard's inert form, I'm numbly aware that his snoring has woken me again. From what I can tell, he snores all night, every night. It's a loud, guttural note with sharp edges and no natural rhythm. I once put my fingers lightly on the bedpost and noticed that the wooden frame actually trembled with each grinding intake of breath. Early in our marriage I just did my best to get to sleep, sometimes lying awake half the night. But then I realised that if I went to bed ahead of Howard, I could fall asleep before his snoring could keep me up. This seems to work most nights, but other times the snoring will wake me. Sometimes Howard's nasal passageways become temporarily blocked. When he finally manages to suck air through, the first snore is really violent… and I wake, fearful and without immediately knowing why. Many years ago I slept in the guest room one night, but Howard was quite upset about that. *A man and women are not meant to sleep in separate beds*, he said. *What sort of marriage is it when husband and wife won't even sleep together*, he said.

I arrive home from work and hear Poppy, our German Shepherd, growling, and I know that Howard is using that oven mitt with her again. Climbing out of the car, I can see them in the backyard – Howard with that oven mitt on, wearing his Bermuda shorts and a t-shirt. Poppy is latched onto that mitt and she's in a frenzy – jerking back and forth, leaping up and down, snarling and foaming at the mouth. Howard looks like he's really struggling with her and there's the usual grimace on his face, but he's silent.

103

I simply do not understand why he does it. I asked him once and he said something about it being fun for Poppy and then mumbled something about training her. It didn't make sense, but I don't bring it up anymore. Howard retired early from the military two years ago. I sometimes wonder if Howard is having a hard time knowing what to do now he hasn't got work anymore. Our two boys moved out as well. Brendan moved to California for a job two years back, and Mitch went to university last year. Howard did everything with our boys. He wouldn't admit it, but I know he misses them.

The physiotherapist introduces himself and offers me his hand. He seems polite and professional, and shows me to his consulting room. The room is pleasant enough – large room-length mirrors on two walls, an examination bed, a changing curtain, a couple of chairs, and some equipment.

"Can you please remove your clothes behind the screen, except your undergarments," he says.

When I emerge from the screen, he says "your family doctor tells me you have restricted movement in your neck and pain in both your right arm and shoulder. What I would like to do is assess the alignment of your posture. Can you please stand with your feet together and with your eyes looking straight ahead, and just relax."

He stands directly in front of me, about 10 feet away, and his eyes move slowly over my body. He then does this from both sides and then from behind. I'm surprised I'm not more self-conscious, but his gaze feels very clinical. Then he does the strangest thing. He takes out a workman's level from a large bag on the floor and holds it across my shoulders from the front and then from the back. Putting the level back into his bag, he presses a thumb into the muscle of my neck, shoulder, and right arm. The pressure increases slowly until I can no longer bear the pain, and when he sees my grimace, he releases the downward force.

"Mrs. Ransom, can you please look at yourself in the mirror straight ahead. Look carefully at your body alignment. What do you see?" I look up and down my body, but everything seems fine.

"I don't see anything unusual. Is there something wrong?"

"Do you feel relaxed at the moment?" he says.

I think about my body. "Yes, I think so."

He then takes a plastic rod from the corner – it must be about 8 feet long – and stands behind me. He reaches around me and holds the rod in front of me, exactly level with my shoulders. I look into the wall-length mirror.

"Jeeezzz." The word escapes from my lips involuntarily.

I can't believe it. The rod might be in line with my shoulders, but it clearly slopes downwards at a bazaar angle. I can see that my right shoulder is much higher than my left. Putting the rod away, he asks me to slowly extend my right arm straight out. My arm doesn't want to go and the pain starts shooting up my neck.

"Mrs. Ransom, the muscles in your right shoulder and upper arm are in a state of chronic tension. Your right shoulder is raised higher than your left because you are tensing these muscles."

"But I didn't even know I was tensing muscles," I say.

"When I asked you if you felt relaxed, you said you were. I believe you *felt* you were relaxed, but people are often unaware of what their bodies are doing. You are chronically tensing the muscles in your right shoulder and upper arm, without knowing that you are doing it. These muscles are constricted and won't relax, and this restricts the movement of your neck, and the muscles eventually become sore from overuse.

"How long have I been doing this for?" My voice sounds small.

"How long have you had soreness in these muscles and restricted movement?"

"It's not always this bad, but... for years."

"Well, that's how long then," he replies.

"But why would I be tensing these muscles?"

"Would you like to put your clothes back on and then perhaps we can talk about this."

When I emerge from behind the screen, he is seated at a table making some notes. He asks me to sit down.

"You want to understand why you have chronically tense muscles in your right shoulder and arm."

"Yes," I say.

"I think this is a very complicated question, but the purpose or function of shoulder and arm muscle is to provide for movement – reaching, holding, grabbing, punching."

"Punching?" I ask.

"Yes, punching is one of the potential functions of an arm. Human beings probably use an arm for punching somewhat less these days, but over 70,000 years of human history punching has been a fairly popular use for an arm. Well, throwing rocks, hitting some animal over the head with a club, throwing a spear." He smiles, but he seems quite serious. "The point is," he continues, "muscles naturally tense when there is an impulse or desire to move them. But if we don't act on that impulse, we are just left with the tension. I assume you are right handed?"

"Yes."

"Well," he says, "you are constricting the muscles in your right arm and shoulder. It's happening for some reason. Why do you think you might be doing that?"

A nervous laugh escapes me. "Well, I certainly don't want to punch anyone."

He stares at me for a moment and finally says, "Okay, I guess it's something to think about. Let's do some work on that shoulder of yours."

He does some pretty deep massage and it hurts like hell, but I'm glad for it somehow. I don't like the pain his hands are causing me, but it's sort of a good pain if it's gonna help with this problem.

I am pulled into consciousness, the bedroom seeming vast and strange. Naturally, the first thing I hear is one of Howard's nasal rippers. Looking at the red numbering on the digital alarm clock I note that it is 2:06 AM, and my heart sinks. Four hours to go before I get up for work. I lie still and try to ignore Howard's snoring. It's impossible. Howard is turned towards my side of the bed and he's almost in the middle of the mattress. Lying with my back to him, I can feel his breath sucking in and out against the cotton of my nightgown, as he gives life to each tearing note.

At 2:37 AM I give up, turn on the small lamp at the desk in the corner of the room, and find my pediatric nursing book. I'm doing some further study to keep my nursing registration up-to-date. The assigned reading reviews different therapeutic approaches to childhood problems. I've learned about Psychoanalysis and just now I'm reading about Behaviorism. The author is explaining something called the *Law of Effect*, which means that whatever follows a behaviour is important. If a behaviour is followed by positive reinforcement, the behaviour is likely to reoccur – if a behaviour is followed by punishment, then the behaviour will be extinguished. As an example, the book discusses the bell and pad method of treating childhood bedwetting. The child is put to bed on a special pad. If the child urinates on the pad, a loud alarm suddenly sounds and the child's sleep is disturbed. Soon, the child learns not to urinate until they wake in the morning, so as not to have their sleep disturbed. Sounds pretty mean, but I suppose it's okay if it works.

Reading about the Law of Effect makes me think about this electric dog collar we have. When Poppy was younger, she was quite difficult. She wouldn't come when you called and she barked a lot. Howard's brother had this electric dog collar which he'd used to train their dog, and he gave it to us. We sat around the dinner table one night, Howard's brother showing us the collar and explaining to us how it worked. I have a memory of dials and buttons and a transmitter. We never even used the thing, but I think I've seen it in our utility room.

I look over at Howard. It's almost 4 AM and his snoring hasn't stopped once. I'm so tired, but my mind is buzzing. I don't decide to get up and head downstairs, my body just seems to do it. Maybe I thought I was going to get a glass of water or perhaps it was for some other reason, but when I'm half-way down the stairs I know I just want to see if that collar is still in the utility room. I turn on a light and open a cupboard, and there it is. It's just like I remembered it. The collar itself is leather and there's this plastic case attached to the collar that you put batteries in. The transmitter is next to it. I open up the battery compartments on the collar and the transmitter and fish out the old batteries. I get some fresh ones from another drawer and fit them in. I still haven't decided what I'm gonna do yet. Ya know, Howard is such a heavy sleeper, he sleeps through thunderstorms. Hell, he *is* a thunderstorm.

I suppose it would be like research, in a way.

I enter our vibrating bedroom, walk to the side of the bed, and gaze down at Howard. I see my hands slowly push the leather collar between his neck and pillow. I'm careful with the small metal studs, but it slides through so easily, so naturally, you would think it was made for Howard rather than Poppy. I fasten the collar and return to my desk chair at the foot of the bed, holding the transmitter on my lap.

My god, what am I doing? This is crazy.

My heart is pumping hard and I can feel a strong throbbing in my temples. I turn off the lamp and now Howard is illuminated by pale moonlight which paints him and the bed sheets in a deep blue. It feels easier in the half-light. I look down at the transmitter. There is this dial with numbers around it – 1 through 10. That must determine how strong the shock will be. I turn the dial to number 1, click a switch to the *on* position, and notice that a red light illuminates. Carefully placing my right thumb over the button, I listen for any rhythm I can discern in his snores.

Don't do it between the snores – only push the button briefly *as* he snores.

My heart bashes itself against my ribcage in staccato rhythm, and I grimace as if I am the one about to receive an electric shock. And then I feel my finger press down. There's a small buzzing noise, but no apparent effect on Howard or his snoring. I try the button at levels 2, 3, 4, and 5, but all that happens is that the buzz gets progressively louder. I can't decide if I'm disappointed or relieved. When I move the dial to 6, the buzz is louder still. Howard's head jerks just a little and his snore is cut right in half – and he stops breathing.

Oh my god, he stopped breathing! I've killed my husband. Oh shit.

But before I can jump up to see if he's all right, he finishes the intake of breath and... for maybe 5 further breaths, he doesn't snore at all. On the sixth breath he snores, but his snore is rather small in stature. But with each successive breath the snores gain in confidence.

What the hell am I doing? What sort of person am I? What if Howard wakes up?

The past few moments suddenly feel like a dream I've just woken from. I quickly turn off the transmitter, carefully remove the collar, and put everything back in the cupboard downstairs. Getting into bed is senseless because I will never be able to get back to sleep, but I find myself climbing quietly under the sheets anyway. Lying in bed feels like where I belong, especially after what I've done.

I find myself thinking about my physio appointment. I don't think I could ever punch anyone.

It's 7 PM and I'm doing the dinner dishes. I look out the window and watch Howard with Poppy in the back yard. Howard is wearing that oven mitt again and Poppy is gripping it hard, jerking her head back and forth violently, snarling. It doesn't make any sense. Howard looks like he's in pain, which does make sense, because it must hurt like hell. God, I feel so tired.

I wake suddenly, and Howard is snoring loudly. I'm shaking all over and I know that I've had an awful dream. I was living with a pack of wild animals – strange creatures, like hyenas, but larger. I was naked and dirty and the pack and I were stalking across what looked like the African Savannah. Then I was in a hospital. In fact, I was a patient at the hospital I work at. A nurse told me that they had to open me up because the wild animals had put poison into me and the surgeon needed to remove it. Suddenly I was aware of the surgeon, who for some reason was standing behind me. I couldn't see who he was because he had a surgical mask on, but he held a long pole. He said that he would open me up, and then use the pole to find the poison.

I can't sleep, I can't read, I don't want to go anywhere, and I don't want to stay here on this vibrating bed. I don't want to think about anything, but my mind won't rest. I want to run somewhere, but I don't know where to go. And suddenly, I feel very alone.

It's harder to get the collar on this time without disturbing Howard because my hands are shaking, but I manage it. What an amusing contradiction: knowing you could stop yourself, knowing you should, and knowing you won't. I sit at the foot of the bed in my desk chair, transmitter antenna pointing at Howard. That same, soft, deep blue moonlight washes over Howard and the bed linen. This time I turn the dial straight to number 6 and wait for the right snore. I remember body surfing as a child and how I watched each wave roll in, waiting for the one which could carry me all the way to the beach. And then my finger presses down. The collar buzzes, and Howard's head jerks slightly and his breath and snore stop, just as before. I want to rush forward to Howard, but I'm less frightened now because I'm pretty sure he will breathe again. He does, and just like the other night he needs a few breaths before his snoring grows to its normal stature. I turn the dial to 7 and push the button just as he starts a big snore. The buzz is louder still, his head jerks, and again his breathing stops. When Howard starts breathing again, I think it takes a whole minute before the snoring begins. Everything feels real and unreal all at once.

I hit Howard with level 7 a few more times, and it takes progressively longer for him to start snoring. Level 8 really zaps him and his head jerks backward even further. His body seems to be adjusting to the shocks because he doesn't stop breathing now, but it is taking longer and longer for him to get his snoring going. Those behaviorists knew what they were doing. But I'm scared. Between the shocks he mumbles and shifts about, making faces. I think he's anticipating the next shock in some way.

Something tells me not to try level 9, but I do. The shock is worse yet, clearly knocking his head backward this time. When the snore is cut off, Howard turns suddenly on his back, grunts, and sits straight up in bed, eyes wide and staring, hands groping into the space in front of him as if he is defending himself. He's staring at me, though I don't think he's aware of me yet.

Oh my God!

I feel an impulse to somehow hide the transmitter and get the collar off, but consciousness is quickly dawning in him and I know this plan is hopeless. And so I just sit very still, transmitter on my lap. Quite suddenly, I know why animals freeze when they are hunted.

"What...? Who...?" says Howard.

And then his gaze comes into focus. When he understands what I'm holding in my hands, he reaches slowly up to his neck and feels the collar. My throat is so constricted, I don't know if I can speak – but I want to try to explain quickly. I put the transmitter down on my desk.

"Howard, I'm so sorry, I don't know why I did it. I just... it was just the snoring and I had been reading about psychology and..."

"You shocked me... you shocked me when I was asleep. How could you do that?"

"Howard, please... ." I move to the edge of the bed. "I'm sorry. I can't believe it myself. It doesn't make any sense... ."

I'm expecting Howard to get mad – who wouldn't, really? But this strange expression comes over his face – a mixture of bewilderment and uncertainty. And then he even smiles a little.

"For Christ sake, Maggie," he finally says, and then he looks like he's at a loss for words. He stares at the bed for a while and eventually says, "come on, I'm tired, let's go back to sleep." He lies down and pulls the sheets up around his neck, and... that's it. He doesn't even take the collar off. I wonder if he really woke up, but he sure seemed awake. I lie down and pull the covers up around my neck. He's even lying down facing in my direction. I want to reach out and put my hand on his shoulder, but decide against it.

Let sleeping dogs lie, I suppose.

I think about Poppy just then, and nothing seems to make any sense.

I was sure Howard was gonna be upset about what happened for a while, but he doesn't even mention it over the next three days. There's something strange about him, though. Every once in a while I look up and find him staring at me, wearing this quizzical expression. It's as if he wants to ask me a question. I'm just hoping the whole thing will go away, and I suppose I try hard to be a good wife – to make up for everything. It's strange – if anything, Howard even seems nicer to me than usual.

I'm sitting up in bed when Howard comes in, gets into his pajamas, and then sits up in bed next to me. I'm really surprised because he doesn't normally come to bed for at least another hour. He has the covers pulled up to his waist and stares down at his hands, folded in his lap.

"You know about the other night... and what happened – you know, with the collar," he says eventually.

"Yes," I reply, and I can feel my breathing quicken with the mention of the subject.

"Well.... ." Howard stares out into space and I can tell he's having an awfully hard time deciding how to say something. I want to help him, but I have no idea where he's going with it. The silence between us buzzes. He can't look at me. He can only stare down at the bed sheets now, searching in vain to find his words. Finally, he opens a drawer in his bedside table and takes out a shiny black wooden club about 12 inches long. It looks like one of those clubs that the English police have. I'm frozen in disbelief as he holds out the club, handle first. I take the club, not knowing what else to do. As the fingers of my right hand curl around the coolness of the handle, I'm surprised at how heavy it is. I can't imagine where he got it from. And then he holds out one hand to me, palm upturned, his eyes still focused on the bedcovers. When he speaks, his voice is small, boyish, and broken.

"If you want to, you can hit me with this. It's okay, if you want to."

And suddenly I know that he wants me to do it. He's serious.

"Okay," I whisper, "but not too hard."

Howard nods his head and extends his palm to me a little further.

Snow in Dubai

I'm sitting inside the Avalanche Café at Ski Dubai, the world's only indoor ski resort. Ski Dubai is an enormous metallic and windowed freezer which sits in the middle of the Arabian Desert, a place as flat and hot as a millpond in hell. Can you believe it? The Avalanche Café sits halfway up the 'ski mountain', and I gaze through a large plate glass window at the 4-person chairlift and the Europeans, East Indians, Japs, and Arabs as they glide past in their colorful ski suits. They keep the temperature at a constant -1 degree, though it seems warmer somehow, maybe because there's no wind indoors. It's a miracle of innovation or an outstanding example of human stupidity, depending on how you look at it.

There's a Talking Heads' song running through my mind, and I find I'm singing it to myself, under my breath. I think it's called *Once in a Lifetime*.

You may find yourself living in another part of the world
You may find yourself behind the wheel of a large automobile
You may find yourself in a beautiful house, with a beautiful wife
You may ask yourself, 'well, how did I get here'?

How *did* I get here? How is it possible that I'm sitting halfway up a fake ski hill, in July, in a café, in Dubai? I pour a little white rum from a small flask I've been hiding from the ski staff into my coffee, and decide I need to think things over. It seems impossible that only 3 years ago I was living with my family in a shitty trailer park on this sun-scorched scrubland in rural South Carolina. My two older brothers are in and out of jail for robbery, assault, and

115

general foolishness, and much to everyone's surprise, I get a place at Carolina State University. So far, so good. I decide I'm gonna do a degree in entrepreneurial studies, which is the sort of degree you probably choose when you come from a trailer park filled with drunks, crack addicts, ex-cons, and every other sort of looser. But before I can make a life for myself, I need to enroll and pay for classes and dorm-room fees – which is a problem because I've got no means to pay. So I did what everyone I ever knew did – I improvised. I used my trailer park connections to sell pot to these rich college kids, who buy the stuff by the garbage bag full. So things are going well, but only for a while, because by the end of my freshman year the college security and local cops are starting to catch on. So I improvised again. I'll spend a year at Richmond University in London, lay low for a while, pick up some course credits, and by the time I get back to Carolina State, I'm old news.

I get to London and realise there's a problem. London is a lot more expensive than I planned on, and I can't figure out how to break into the dope market there. So I'm running out of money by the end of the first semester and doing some serious head-scratching when I meet these Bulgarians in a pub. We have a few beers and get to talking. These guys are bringing in cocaine – Columbia to America to Amsterdam to England – and they need a fresh-faced college kid to sell the stuff on-site. So I start selling cocaine to rich British college kids, who buy the stuff by the bin bag.

My train of thought is broken by the sight of this beautiful girl I notice through the café window. She's skiing down the hill, fairly slowly, but with a nice rhythm, keeping her skis close together. She's got blue muffs over her ears, and long blond hair which swings behind her with every turn. She's at the bottom of the hill now and I lose sight of her as she joins the back of the cue for the chair lift.

So I was settling into London, selling coke, paying for my courses and textbooks, and generally keeping my head down. *Trailer park kid makes good, and all that.* But then my contacts told me that their boss wanted to meet me. I had a bad feeling about it, but I couldn't really say no. So I met in the back room of a pub with a guy named Bogdan, another Bulgarian, and one of the fattest people I'd ever seen. He thanked me for my services, told me he was happy with my work, and wanted to know if I'd like to 'make some real money'. I told Bogdan that I was grateful for everything but that I was pretty happy with our current arrangement, which was true, but it was like he didn't even hear me. He started telling me about this new job I was going be doing for him. 'It's really simple,' he said. 'Twice a month you fly to Dubai and meet up with a guy named Viktor. Viktor will give you some cash, and you just follow the instructions Viktor gives you. 'What sort of instructions?' I asked Bogdan. 'Well,' he said, 'you deposit the money in a Dubai bank, and you might purchase a property once in a while.' I told Bogdan I was very flattered, but that I was pretty happy just selling the coke. Bogdan smiled and said, 'that's okay, you're gonna like your new job a lot more,' and he bought me another drink and started asking me about American football. Apparently he was a fan of the Washington Redskins because their uniform used the same shade of red as the Bulgarian flag.

That gorgeous girl is getting off the chairlift at the top of the hill. She rode the lift with three Japanese guys, but I can tell she's alone by the way she skis away from them. I really like the blue jacket and matching ski pants she's wearing. It complements her pale skin and blond hair. She looks about 20, maybe 22. And then, just as she passes by, she looks up. Her expression is impassive, giving nothing away, but she looks straight at me. My heart is pounding all of a sudden. I lose her again in the chairlift line.

I was hoping my meeting with Bogdan had been some strange Bulgarian joke, but two weeks later I met with my contacts, and instead of my usual supply of coke, they gave me 5,000 dollars US, a return plane ticket to Dubai International Airport, and an address for Viktor. Shit. Any sense of self-preservation I possessed should have immediately kicked in, and I should have got on the first plane back to South Carolina. But the truth is, no one had ever paid me that sort of money... and just for making a delivery. I had to admit, I was excited and intrigued. Five days later, I was exiting Dubai airport and walking around the city, trying to find Viktor's apartment. I was amazed at what I saw. Everything about Dubai shimmered in stark sunshine. The metallic and glassed skyscrapers, the white sand beaches, the walkways, the blue sky and even bluer Indian Ocean. Everything looked like it had been born yesterday. After spending the past 6 months in overcast and dirty London, I felt like I was on a different planet. I was overawed, and shitting my pants.

Viktor let me into his modest apartment and invited me to sit on his couch. He made us tea without asking if I wanted any, and sat across from me. He looked like he'd spent half his life working out with weights. Bulging muscles stretched the fabric of t-shirt and jeans. But he looked nervous, fumbling with matches as he lit up a cigarette.

"You want a cigarette?" he asked.

"No thanks, Viktor." Viktor smoked his cigarette and looked me over.

"So are you Bulgarian?" I asked.

"Naturally," he said, smiling.

"So Bogdan tell you what you gonna do?" said Viktor.

"Bogdan just told me to meet with you and that you would give me some money and instructions."

"That's right," said Viktor. He went into another room and returned with a suitcase, which he put on a coffee table between us. He opened it up and I almost choked on my tea. The case was filled with stacks of cash, each stack with a rubber band around it. I saw US Dollars, British Pounds, Euros, Russian Roubles, and currency I didn't recognize.

"We count it together," said Viktor, "and you go to the bank, open an account, and deposit the money."

"Viktor, are you kidding? There's got to be hundreds of thousands of dollars in there. How can I just put that into a bank?"

"Why the fuck do you think we in Dubai?" he'd said. "Dubai don't give a fuck where you get your money or how much you got, just as long as you put it into their banks. You just show them your passport, open an account, and deposit the money. It's easy."

"If it's so easy, then why doesn't Bogdan just have you deposit the money?"

"I probably could," said Viktor. "But Dubai likes Americans more than Bulgarians. America has got too much money invested in Dubai."

And Viktor was right. The bank clerk who opened the account for me looked entirely board as he'd counted the equivalent of 462,328 thousand US dollars, and then handed me a bank book and receipt. And so it went. Every two weeks I was given a cash payment and a plane ticket, flew to Dubai, drank tea and counted money with Viktor, made a deposit, and occasionally withdrew money and bought a house in some upscale Dubai suburb. I think I own 12 houses now, which earn a lot of rent, all of which goes back to Bogdan, of course. Eighteen months later I'm still in London, trying to collect credits at Richmond College, which is tough when you have to skip certain classes because Bogdan decides it's time to make a trip to Dubai. It should be easier by now, but I'm still scared every time I go through customs and enter the bank. I wish Viktor weren't so damn nervous.

Fucking Dubai. My first impression was way off. Dubai, as it turns out, is a glittering shit-hole. Radiant on the surface, rotten at the core. The Dubai Centre for Commerce and Tourism boasts of *outstanding financial services*. It's crap. What they mean is that Dubai is a massive money laundering machine. Dubai sits on a migratory path between Europe, Asia, and Africa. Stop in, deposit your money, invest your money, enjoy the sunshine and beach, and come back soon. You may have to put up with a few minor inconveniences. Please don't mention homosexuality or the theory of evolution, and you'll find some internet sites blocked, like dating networks, gay and lesbian sites, all sites originating from Israel, and anything critical of the United Arab Emirates. But with so much money to be made, so what? And why does Dubai not care where your money came from? Because these Arabs want to beat the Western world at their own game. And they're actually doing it. Western cash has meant that Dubai now has the world's tallest building, the world's largest shopping mall, the world's largest man-made harbour, the world's most expensive hotel, and don't forget, the world's only indoor ski resort. Hooray for Dubai. God, how I hate this place.

The girl begins another run down the hill, slow and smooth. Some Jap kids are bombing past her on snowboards, shouting at one another, but she ignores them. Man, is she gorgeous. She veers off her normal course and I lose site of her because she skis around the other side of Avalanche café.

After I'd made several deposits in the Dubai bank, my London contacts told me that Bogdan wanted to meet me again. I was worried that I'd made some mistake, but that wasn't it. Bogdan bought me a drink at the same pub we first met, but now he's brought along a couple of goons, and all I can remember about them is that they looked bored and had a lot of thick, dark arm hair.

"So, everything go okay cowboy?" he asked. I guess cowboy had become my new nickname.

"Yeah, everything is fine."

120

"Good," said Bogdan, and then he gave me a long calculating look.

"You must wonder where all that money came from, no?" he said. Of course I'd wondered, but I hadn't really wanted to know. It had to be trafficking. I already knew they moved cocaine, but I didn't want to know anymore.

"I haven't thought about that much," I said.

"Well," said Bogdan. "You're one of us now, so you should know." I didn't want to be one of them, I didn't want to be part of their chummy Bulgarian brotherhood, and I didn't want to know anything... but I wasn't about to tell Bogdan that.

"You like women, don't you cowboy?"

Shit, I thought. It was women then. I stared at him impassively.

"Everyone likes women," continued Bogdan. "You ever heard of *The Road of Shame*?"

"Bogdan, maybe I don't need to know everything."

"No, no..." said Bogdan. "You gonna find this interesting." He smiled before continuing. "The Road of Shame is this stretch of highway which links Dresden, Prague and Czechoslovakia. It was a bad time for a lot of people, and young Czech women, mostly gypsies, started selling themselves along the E55, mostly to fat Germans. Those Germans would no longer have to go all the way to the Far East for sex tourism anymore – now they could get it on their doorstep. It was so popular that there weren't nearly enough Czech lovelies for all those sweaty Germans in their BMWs and lorries. So down in Sofia, we thought, now there's a business, and why should Czech gypsies have all the fun. There are unlucky beautiful women from everywhere – Romania, Bulgaria, Serbia, Ukraine. You see?" Maybe I didn't see everything, but I saw more than I wanted to. Bogdan and his goons trafficked women from every depressed and chaotic region of Eastern Europe.

But what I didn't understand was why Bogdan was telling me this. And that worried me, so a couple of weeks later, I'm down in

Dubai, sitting across a coffee table and counting money with Viktor, and I asked him about it.

"Bogdan told you about the women?" he said.

"Yeah."

"Well, I guess that means your one of us now," he said, smiling. I clenched my teeth and exhaled heavily, trying not to let my irritation show.

"But why would Bogdan tell me where the money was coming from," I said.

Viktor smiled again. "Bogdan told you because now he knows that you know that he knows." Viktor must have noticed the look of confusion on my face, because he continued. "Now you're... how do you say it? Implicated. Your part of what we do. Understand?"

"Shit," I said under my breath.

"It also means," continued Viktor, "that you work for Bogdan directly now – see?"

"No," I said, a sense of panic crawling up my abdomen. "I don't see." And I was irritated as well as scared. Organized crime is a pain in the ass because no one says anything directly.

Viktor smiled, and I thought I saw a glimmer of amusement in his expression. "When you work for Bogdan," he said slowly, "you work for Bogdan for as long as Bogdan needs you."

I closed my eyes and exhaled a large breath of air. I looked up. "Viktor, is Bogdan going to kill me someday?"

Viktor broke out laughing and it took him about a minute to compose himself. "I don't know," he said finally, and he seemed to be speaking frankly. "But if you decide to go home, Bogdan can find you in South Carolina."

I stared at Viktor, open-mouthed and fence-post stupid. I was shocked that Viktor knew here I had come from. I'd never even given my Bulgarian contacts in London that information.

I am suddenly aware that this beautiful girl is standing at the entrance of the café, looking around the room. I wonder if she's looking for someone, or just choosing an empty table. I'm nervous at seeing her, but pleased she's here. I try not to stare. A moment later she heads in my direction and then unzips her ski jacket, which she places on the back of a chair at the table next to mine. She goes to the bar and makes her order, speaking good English, but with an exotic accent. She is wearing a white undergarment which I notice in detail. I gulp too hard on my coffee, and my throat hurts momentarily. She returns to her table with a hot chocolate piled high with whipped cream. She has chosen to sit directly opposite me at her table and I pretend to study my coffee cup. I realise quite suddenly that if I do not speak to her, I will never forgive myself. And yet, how to start a conversation without sounding like some creepy, lonely pervert? I look up at her.

"You're quite a good skier," I say. I point out the window. "I couldn't help noticing you when you came down the hill." She smiles and laughs faintly.

"No, I'm not too good. I'm learning."

"Well, it's my first time skiing, so you are much better than I am." There's a pause in our conversation, and she looks away. Come on, don't give up now.

"My name is Henry, but people call me Hank. I'm American. I hope you don't mind me talking to you."

"No – I don't mind," she says matter-of-factly.

"You speak good English. Do you mind if I ask where you are from?"

"Ukraine. A small town outside of Kiev."

"Ah, I bet they have lots of snow for skiing where you come from?" She looks at her hot chocolate thoughtfully.

"Yes, a lot of snow, but most of the Ukraine is flat."

"Are there no mountains at all?" I ask.

She nods. "In the East there are the Carpathian Mountains and in the South the Crimean... but my family was very poor."

"Oh," I say, feeling somewhat disarmed. "That's okay. My family was poor too."

"I thought you said you were an American."

"I am," I say. "We have poor people in America too."

"I bet not like Ukraine."

"Really," I say smiling. "I bet my family was poorer than yours."

She laughs. "Did your family have a TV set?"

"Yes," I acknowledge.

"You lose then," she says, smiling broadly, exposing teeth which are very white, but crooked. Crooked teeth like that on so beautiful a girl would simply not exist in America, but to me her teeth make her even more beautiful.

"What's your name?" I ask.

She pauses and looks uncertain. "It's Anastasia," she says, finally.

"That's beautiful," I say. She smiles shyly.

"I have to go to the toilet," she says, looking around the room. She spots the toilet and walks off, glancing back at me briefly. I notice she's left her ski jacket and those blue ear muffs, which is reassuring. I feel an impulse to reach over and touch her blue ear muffs for some strange reason.

I pull my cell phone out of my pocket and open up Wikipedia. I knew this guy back at Carolina State University who discovered this terrific way to impress girls. After he got their name, he'd look up the name on his cell phone. And then later he'd say something to the girl like, 'so your name is Emma, I think that's originally German, isn't it? Doesn't it mean something like universal or all-containing'? Emma, or whomever it might be, was invariably impressed. She imagined this guy to be very smart and cultured, when in fact he was merely clever and underhanded.

I type Anastasia into my cell phone, and a moment later read, *Anastasia, originally from the Greek, meaning resurrection...* I stare at those words, feeling mildly stunned and unable to absorb the full meaning of this discovery. Resurrection, I whisper under my breath, sensing the word vibrate slightly just beneath my skull. I am jerked out of a reflective trance by the site of Anastasia as she exits the ladies' room. She sits down in her chair and takes a spoonful of whipped cream from the hot chocolate into her mouth. A bit of whipped cream remains on her lip, which she is unaware of. I like her even more for that bit of whipped cream – every little imperfection seems to somehow make her more attractive. I put my phone in my pocket. I have no intention of pretending to know the origin of her name.

I point to her blue ear muffs on the table. "I like your ear muffs. They're sort of funny."

She puts her ear muffs on her head and smiles. "They're warm," she says.

A sudden whooshing noise becomes audible, and we look out the window. The skiing has finished for the day and the resort has turned on the artificial snowmakers, tall metal tubes that spurt a fine, misty type of snow onto the slopes.

It's different than real snow, isn't it," says Anastasia. "I mean snow which falls from the sky." She looks at me. "Do they have snow where you lived?"

"I come from South Carolina – it's too hot for snow where I grew up. But I did see real snow once. I was 14-years-old and I ran away from home. I got on a bus and went to the Blue Ridge Mountains because I'd seen pictures of those mountains and I wanted to see them for real."

"What happened?" she asks.

"I started out at the base of a mountain and spent all day climbing it. It was really beautiful and I was alone and I felt really good – you know, free, like I was doing something amazing. I made it nearly to the top of the mountain by evening. I made a fire, ate some dinner and got into my sleeping bag. In the middle of the night, I woke up and my face felt really wet and cold. I sat up and saw the most beautiful thing. Everything – the pine trees, the mountains – was lit up by a full moon, and these huge snowflakes were falling down, really slowly."

"Yes..." says Anastasia reflectively. "Do you know what I'd really like to do someday?"

"What's that?" I ask.

"I'd like to go skiing on real snow, on a real mountain, in the Alps. To stay at one of those chalets and ski every day."

"That sounds great," I say.

She suddenly looks at her wrist watch. "I have to go to work – I can't be late." She begins to collect her blue ear muffs and jacket hurriedly.

"Anastasia," I say. I can't believe she is simply going to leave. We stare at one another for a moment, until she understands that I don't know what to say.

"Hank," she says, but she manages to pronounce it Henk. "You are nice, but I have to go to work now."

"Look," I stammer. "I have to return to London early tomorrow morning. Where do you work? Can I see you?"

She gazes at me, studying our situation with what seems like a sad and bleak precision. "You want to see me," she says, emphasizing the words *see me* in a strange manner.

"Yes," I say.

She pauses, thoughtfully. "I work at Cyclone," she says. She stands up, turns quickly and takes a few steps before stopping. She turns and looks back at me. "I ran away from home once too," she says, and a moment later she is gone.

I return to my hotel, take a shower, and have a talk with the desk manager. Cyclone, I discover, is a nightclub. Situated in Bur

Dubai, just across the creek from Deira, it's a 15-minute walk for me. By 10:15 PM, I'm standing in a short cue at the entrance to the club, and I can't help feeling intimated. The club is quite upscale. Everyone is receiving a brief frisking by polite uniformed security guards as they pass through, and I realize two things. One, all the clientele are men, and two, I'm the only one not wearing a suit coat. Shit.

"Good evening boss," the guard says to me cheerily as he moves his hands with quick and professional confidence over my chest, waist, back, and down my thighs. He glances at an attendant standing nearby and nods his head. The attendant disappears and reappears a moment later holding a cheap blue blazer, which he hands to the guard.

"You will need this boss," he says, offering me both a smile and the blazer. "Just return it on your way out please. Have a good evening."

I enter the main room and look around, my eyes taking some time to adjust to the low lighting. There are numerous tables, a dance floor, a DJ, and two bars. About 75% of the tables are occupied, and I settle into one of the booths near the back of the room. The Arab DJ is playing a Madonna track and a few couples are dancing. Most of the tables are occupied by men, some in pairs, but quite a lot of men are on their own. Staff move about the tables carrying trays and drinks, but I don't see Anastasia among them. In fact, all the staff – bartenders, waiters, security – seem to be men. Then I notice something odd about the two kidney-bean shaped bars. There are a few men standing around the bars, but there must be a couple of dozen women at each bar. Women at the bars – men at the tables. It reminds me of those odd school dances I went to as a kid where the boys and girls lined up on either side of a decorated gymnasium. But there's something else which is strange – all the woman at the bar to my left are oriental, and the woman at the other bar are white. A young

Chinese woman approaches my table, wearing a shimmering short dress and a solicitous smile.

"Hello. Do you like me?" She leans forward and places her palms on my table, partially exposing small breasts. "I can give you very good sex. Only 400 Dirham."

"No thank you. I'm… looking for someone."

"Oh," she says, a sad pout forming on her recently pubescent face. "You have special girl?"

"No," I say in a strangely defensive manner. "I just don't… I'm sorry… I'm just not interested right now."

As the Chinese girl makes her way back to her bar, I scan the room again. No Anastasia. An Arab waiter approaches.

"Hello Sir. What drink will you have?" I order a beer and he returns a couple of minutes later with my drink.

"Thirty-five Dirham please," he says. Christ – 8 dollars for a beer. But I give him 50 Dirham and tell him to keep the change. He is clearly pleased by the unexpected tip.

"Excuse me," I say, before he has a chance to move to another customer.

"This is my first time at Cyclone. The women at the bars… they are… for sale?"

"Yes sir," he says.

"Why are all the oriental woman at one bar and all the white women at the other?"

"It's better that way," he says. "Sometimes there were fights. The Chinese woman always try to charge less money, and that makes the Russian and Ukrainian woman upset, so we made two bars."

Ukrainian women, I thought. Anastasia. The waiter smiles and leaves me for another customer. The reality of my situation is becoming difficult to deny, and I try in desperation to sift through a kaleidoscope of feelings. I take a few big swallows of beer and rub my eyes hard with the palms of my hands. I watch as young

women, invariably clothed in short glittering dresses and high-heels, talk and dance with the clients. As deals are struck, I see couples take to a flight of stairs leading up to what must be private rooms. I think about Bogdan, the image of his fat greasy face hovering before me. *You like women, don't you cowboy?*
Fuck. I don't know what to do. I could leave now – maybe that would be best, for both of us. And then I see her. She's walking down the stairs with a gracefulness strangely reminiscent of the way she skied down the slopes this afternoon. She's wearing a blue dress, shimmering in the sparse lighting, and she is utterly beautiful. At that moment, all the confused feelings and impulses dissolve into nothing, and I understand one thing – I don't care about any of this. As she approaches the bottom of the steps, I stand up to get a clearer view over the heads of the patrons. Our eyes meet, and she stops, seemingly frozen. She looks over at the bar, then back to me, as if making a decision. She seems to exhale a large breath of air, and a moment later she is walking towards my table.

She is there in front of me, her stance simple and open, smiling sadly. "You wanted to see me," she says. She opens her arms and turns her palms up, then motions to the tables, dance floor, and bars behind her. "Look." She says this single word in a plain and frank manner, as if leaving me at liberty to make sense of her remark. I can feel my heart hammering against my chest and I struggle to stay in control, fight to know the right thing to say.

"Can you sit down for a minute?" Anastasia looks over her shoulder briefly, and then slides into the booth.

"Anastasia, I don't care about any of this," I say, motioning to the room. "I don't care what you've done – I'm sure there are reasons…"

She gazes at me, her expression impassive, and I feel lost. I would just have to continue. I pull from my pocket the piece of paper I had printed off the hotel's printer after I had my shower, after I had done some research on the computer which came with my room. I unfold the paper and smooth the creases against the table. "Look at this," I say.

Anastasia peers through the half-light, taking her time to absorb the photos and read the printed information. My heart continues to bash against my chest, and I feel desperate for her to talk, to say something. At last she looks up, an expression of confusion on her face.

"This is a ski resort in France. Why are you showing me this?"

"Look," I say, pointing to a photo displaying mountainous ski slopes. "This is Chamrousse, it's a big ski resort in the Alps. It's beautiful, isn't it? Real snow. And this," I say, pointing to another photo, "is the ski chalets they have right on the mountain. In the morning you wake up, have a hot breakfast, and just ski straight out the front door! We can go there, together. We can stay and ski for as long as we feel like it."

Anastasia's eyes narrow, and a look of irritation comes over her. "So you are going to save me then? Take me away from this. You know, you are not the first man who wants to rescue me."

"No, it's not like that."

"You don't even know me," she says.

"I know that, but… it's not that I want to rescue you. It's different."

She laughs in what seems like disbelief. "Henk…" she says. I was quite sure I didn't want to listen to what was coming next, but I was very pleased to hear her use my name. "… You want me to repair your soul then."

"What?" I ask.

"You want me to repair your soul, don't you?"

"No," I protest, and then I find that we were suddenly staring at one another, and I am desperately afraid that there is nothing left to say. I gaze out at the room because I find it difficult to look at her. The DJ is getting very excited about something, the place is filling up with more men, and I notice the Chinese girl I had met earlier ascending the stairway with a large businessman. I look back to Anastasia.

"Yes, you're right. I'd like you to help repair my soul, if that's how you want to put it. And I want to help repair yours." It was all I had left, and I think it was true.

She laughs and smiles, shaking her head. "That's not how it works."

"Why not?" I insist.

"Because that's not what happens," she says, a terse edge slipping into her tone. She looks around the room and then back at me. "You are a nice boy Henk. If you want to go upstairs, we can. Just 200 Dirham."

"No," I say, a feeling of disbelief taking hold. She begins to slide out of the booth. I stare at her with what must appear a pathetic and pleading expression, but I can't help myself. She shakes her head and laughs again.

"I'm sorry, but I have to go." She takes a few steps and then turns, placing a hand on one hip. She shakes her head, a quizzical expression forming. "Why are you saying all of this?"

I open my mouth to speak, but I can't find any words. She turns quickly, and as she walks away I notice that she doesn't wear high-heels like the other girls. Instead, on her feet are something like sparkly sneakers, which seem out of place. That makes me a little more depressed because I realise it's just one more reason to like her.

I decide to stick around. I'm all dressed up in my borrowed suit coat and out on the town. I might as well get a bit drunk, stare into the middle distance, and wallow in self-pity. I finish a couple more beers, barely aware of the growing din of enthusiasm around me. I don't look for Anastasia, but the place had filled up with so many patrons that it's unlikely I'd see her anyway. Just after midnight I find myself gazing abstractly at the promotional information about the French ski resort. I notice that the bottom third of the page is blank, and I fumble in my pocket for a pen. I'm a little drunk, so I need to steady my hand and concentrate as I write:

Why am I saying all this?

I consider what to write next. Because you're beautiful? Because you make me laugh? Because you're special? It's all true and it all sounds like bullshit. But worse, it doesn't do my feelings justice. So I add:

Because I love you.

Underneath, I write the name and address of my hotel. On the way out, I return my blazer to the doorman. I hold out the note and ask if he will give it to Anastasia. I'm aware of the senselessness of my gesture, but I'm fairly sure I've already forfeited every means of dignity, so there seems little reason to stop now. The doorman accepts the note but doesn't look very happy about it. It occurs to me that the patrons of Cyclone probably hand him notes all the time and that he is likely to see me as just another guy caught up in some net of confusion and desire. He's probably right.

I walk out onto the pavement and lean against the brick of the club. The bass of dance music vibrates through my back, the effects of the beer vibrate through my head, and I try to remember how to get back to my hotel. I look up into the darkness. It's very likely that the night sky is clear, but you can never be sure because you can't see the stars – the lights of Dubai are too bright.

"Hey buddy," I hear a voice call. It's an Arab who's just come out of the club. He's staggering towards me, a sloppy grin on his face, his suit coat wrinkled, shirt untucked. "Hey buddy" he says, putting a hand on my shoulder and breathing in my face. "You American?"

"Yeah, I American," I say.

"Yeah, you American. I can see. America…" he says, leaning into me for support. "Kyle Minogue, yeah, she one hot hottie, yeah. Wooo America!"

"Kyle Minogue isn't American," I say. "She's Australian."

He looks confused. "Kyle Minogue is Austrian?"

"No," I say. "She's Au –strai-lian."

He slaps me on the shoulder and leans right against me before pushing himself upright, using the wall for support. His breath stinks of some unnamable mixture of booze and cigarettes. He must be one of those *new* Muslims, but whatever he is, I just wish he'd get off me.

"Hey buddy, you hear they pay Kyle Minogue a lot of millions to sing at the Atlantis." I'd read about that. Some stupid-ass Dubai Sheik is gonna pay out 4.4 million so Kyle Minogue can sing and shake her ass for the opening of a new shopping mall.

"Yeah, I heard," I say, pushing him away from me quite hard. "Sounds like a fucking bargain." He staggers backwards and stumbles, almost falling.

"Hey buddy," he says, surprised that I shoved him just when we were doing such a good job of this drunken male bonding thing. "No problem Buddy," he says. "Okay." He looks a little hurt and scared, and I feel bad I shoved him.

"Yeah, it's okay. Look, I'm Sorry," I say, raising my hands.

He nods, a sour expression forming around his mouth and eyes, and staggers off down the street to a life I'm sure I don't understand at all. I lean against the brick and look up into the sky, or the street lights rather. And I find that I'm remembering more of that Talking Heads song, which I sing under my breath.

You may ask yourself, 'What is that beautiful house?'
You may ask yourself, 'Where does that highway lead to?'
You may ask yourself, 'Am I right, am I wrong?'
You may say to yourself, 'My God, what have I done?'

I think about Anastasia. I think about the plane I have to catch tomorrow morning, my Bulgarian contacts in London, Bogdan, and the plane back to Dubai I'll have to catch in a couple of weeks. I shove my hands into my pockets and trudge slowly towards my hotel, a single thought taking hold of me: *My God, what have I done?*

I wake the following morning with a slight headache, roll out of bed, and gaze through the large plate glass window of my 10th floor hotel room. There is Dubai, winking skyscrapers and tidy roads dazzling in the morning sunshine. The air-conditioning keeps the room at a comfortable 70 degrees, but the orange heat shimmers off the pavements below, and I can tell it's gonna be a scorcher. Despite all the technology and industrial refinements, it's still a goddamned desert.

I exit the elevator in the main lobby and approach the desk, a small luggage bag trailing behind me. The attendant is busy with a phone call, so I stare into the large mirror behind him. My mouth drops open involuntarily. Reflected in the mirror is a young blond woman sitting on a seat, wearing a t-shirt, shorts, and blue ear muffs. Next to her is a large suitcase. She smiles at me, revealing a beautiful set of crooked white teeth. Strangely, I am a little afraid to turn around, worried that she won't be there.

I sit next to Anastasia, and we smile at one another shyly.

"You came," I say.

"Yes.... I'm sorry I didn't believe you."

The blue ear muffs look very silly in the desert Summertime of Dubai.

"You wore your ear muffs?"

"Of course," she says. "It's for skiing in France." We share a laugh, which seems to break the tension.

"I'm really glad you came."

She looks down for a moment, thoughtfully. "So am I," she says. "But there is something you should know if we are really going away together."

"What is it?" I ask.

"There are people here in Dubai who are not going to be happy if I leave."

"Oh," I say. "Well, there are people in London and in Bulgaria who are not going to be happy if I disappear. We just have to stick together, and everything will be okay."

She nods her head and I think we both understand that it's better not to talk about it any further – at least not now.

We step out of the cab at Dubai International Airport. We had tried to make a little small talk with the cabbie during the trip, but he didn't seem to have much English. I'm thinking about buying tickets for France as we stand at the trunk of the car, waiting for the Arab driver to help us with our luggage. I stopped in at a bank and borrowed some money from Bogdan before we got our cab, which is probably a terrible idea. I'm a little worried about my family and friends in South Carolina, but I think there's a good chance that even hardened Bulgarians will get their asses kicked by the white trailer park types I grew up with. My brothers aren't even in jail at the moment. I hope everyone will be okay, but as mean as those Bulgarians seem, you'd have to be crazy to fuck with the residents of Oak Ridge Trailer Park. I make a mental note to give my family a call before we get on the plane.

"Look," I hear Anastasia say. She's pointing into the air.

I see small white flecks falling slowly to the ground. We look at one another, confusion marking our faces.

"What is it?" I say.

Anastasia smiles and shrugs. "I don't know, but it looks like snow."

"That's impossible," I say. "It must be 110 degrees."

The cabbie had pulled our bags from the car, and I thank and tip him. I point to the sky. "Do you know what that is... falling from the sky." He doesn't understand me, so I point again, wiggling my fingers in a downward motion. He smiles and points into the distance at two large factory chimneys.

"Qism alShurtah alBareed," he says.

Anastasia grabs my arm. "I think he said it's a plastics factory. They make something plastic and this stuff comes out of the chimneys."

"Oh," I say. "The wind must blow it here."

She squeezes my arm. "It's Dubai snow," she says, and we laugh together.

"Is funny?" the cabbie says, finding some English after all.

I smile at him. "It's a complicated story." He returns my smile, shakes our hands, and drives off. We watch the falling white bits of plastic fluff for a moment longer.

"Let's get out of this place," I say. Anastasia nods, takes my hand, and we walk together towards the airport entrance.

#0327 - 290316 - C0 - 229/152/0 - PB - DID1403913